THE LOVE
YOU CRAVE

John Locke is a *New York Times* bestselling author, and was the first self-published author in history to hit the number 1 spot on Kindle. He is the author of the Donovan Creed and Emmett Love series. He lives in Kentucky.

JOHN LOCKE

***** Worthy of 6 Stars! By TRW

I give 5 stars to all John Locke books. I would give 6 stars to this one if I could. Not only is it a page turning thriller – I read the whole thing on the beach in an afternoon – couldn't put it down.

***** A fun read! By Kathy

This novel is chock-full of surprising plot twists and turns from beginning to end. It grips you from page one. I read this book in one evening. It's a fast, fun read for sure.

***** Bingo! Cool. Read this book and you're hooked on Locke. By Karin

Locke keeps the story moving and in such an effortless way. I'm passing it on to my husband. It's been awhile since I've read something sexy: this fits the bill.

***** So Entertaining I just went and downloaded another one. By Patti Roberts

I read this book over a period of 2 days on my Kindle and loved it! So I have just downloaded another one. I hereby declare that I am a John Locke fan. Do yourself a favor....

***** Life equals Experimentation. By Jean I just couldn't put the book down. Must Read!

***** 10 stars. By Ally

A wonderful mystery thriller. I love all of them but I think this is just my favorite.

***** I loved this book. By D Loewe
I don't write reviews, I just don't. But after reading this book I enjoyed it so much I felt the author deserved a positive review. I will not go into the plot or such, but I could not put this thing down. Well done Mr. Locke and thank you.

***** OMG!! By Kimberly Morris
What a ride...wow. The first jaw falling open moment in a book that I recall ever having experienced.

*****5 out of 5 stars. By Mr C. Headle
I thought Lethal People was amazing so I read Lethal Experiment and officially became addicted to the series. A marvel combination of action, drama, and breath-taking excitement. I love how Donovan Creed constantly keeps us wanting more. Do yourself a favor and grab this book!

***** Don't even bother trying to catch your breath! By Karin Gambaro
From the moment I started reading this book, I was hooked on Donovan Creed! This was my first Donovan Creed experience, and I can't wait to dive into the rest of the series. This guy is the hero I've been waiting for! Thanks, John Locke!

*****Incredible! By Amethyst
Man oh man alive. Donovan Creed is an absolutely perfect character.

AMAZON.COM

THE DONOVAN CREED SERIES

THE LOVE
YOU CRAVE
JOHN LOCKE

HEAD
of ZEUS

This edition first published in the UK in 2013 by Head of Zeus Ltd

9 7 5 3 1 2 4 6 8

A CIP catalogue record for this book is available from
the British Library.

ISBN (Paperback): 9781781852446
ISBN (eBook): 9781781852453

Printed and bound by CPI Group (UK) Ltd, Croydon, CR0 4YY

Head of Zeus Ltd
Clerkenwell House
45-47 Clerkenwell Green
London EC1R 0HT

www.headofzeus.com

THE LOVE YOU CRAVE

PROLOGUE

WHEN CALLIE CARPENTER'S cell phone vibrated on her nightstand a single time she leaped out of bed and threw on some clothes.

"What're you doing?" said Gwen, her bedmate.

"I'm on alert."

"What's that mean?"

Callie raced to the bathroom, relieved herself, brushed her teeth, grabbed her car keys.

"It means Creed might need me. If he does, he'll call back. If he does, he's in trouble. If he is, I could be in trouble."

"I'm coming with you."

"Not on your life."

"You can't stop me!"

"Get real," Callie said.

"What about me?" Gwen said, pouting.

"What about you?"

"I want to feel useful."

Callie sighed. "Go to the guest bedroom. Set out a scarf, a vibrator, and five random items. Doesn't matter what they are, as long as they fit on the counter."

"Why?"

"I'll tell you later."

"Where are you going?"

"To the car. I need to be on the street, engine running,

ready to roll."

"Sounds like that man has you wrapped around his little finger."

"Don't start with me."

1.

Donovan Creed

HERE'S SOMETHING YOU don't see every day.

I'm jogging south on Las Vegas Boulevard, four miles south of the Strip, when a lady walks right smack into a lamp post.

She's on Trace Street, forty yards to my right. I stop in the middle of the intersection to look and see if she's okay. It's five a.m., and from my angle and distance I could be wrong about what I thought I saw. She backs up a few steps and falls to a seated position on the sidewalk.

I wonder if she's drunk.

I scan the area to see if anyone else is watching this unfold, but see no one. We're in an industrial area, no bars nearby, and no businesses are open on Trace. I want to finish my run, but can't leave her sitting there if she's hurt. On the other hand, I don't want to get shot. It was just last week a Vegas woman staggered out of a bar in the wee hours of the morning when some local thug took her for an easy mark and got killed for his miscalculation.

She's sitting with her back to me, so all I get is the shadow view. Her handbag is lying beside her. If it contains a gun, it won't take her long to reach it.

Thirty yards beyond the seated lady, a van slowly comes into view at the next intersection and pulls to a stop. So it's me at this intersection, the van at the next, and a lady sitting between us, on the sidewalk. The van is white, with the passenger side facing the lady, but it's dark and too far away for me to make out any details.

I don't know how many people are in the van, but I'm guessing just the driver. I mean, a passenger would roll the window down and ask if she needs help, right?

The van driver seems to be doing what I'm doing, staring at the woman. But he's got a better view, the illuminated front side of her. We're probably both waiting to see if she's going to stand, and we're probably both leery about getting shot. In my case, I'm unarmed.

Well, that's not completely true. I have my cell phone in my hand. In an emergency, I can press a button, fling it, and two seconds later it blows up.

But I don't press that button. Instead, I press a number that rings Callie's phone a single time. She's now on alert.

I start walking toward the lady.

"Miss!" I yell, loud enough for her to hear. "Are you okay?"

I wonder why people always ask that. Of course she's not okay. She just walked into a friggin' lamp post! But that's what people always ask. A little kid falls into a well and gets stuck twenty feet below the surface. "Are you okay?" people shout.

She's not okay.

Before I cover ten yards, her head explodes.

I stop in my tracks and instinctively drop to the ground to make myself a smaller target. I'm so stunned I hardly notice the van slowly backing out of view. But the fact it's backing up instead of racing forward tells me whoever's in the van had something to do with the lady's head exploding. And the way the street light hits the front of the van as it's backing up

4

shows me something I hadn't seen before: a magnetic sign on the side, above the front wheel well. I can't make out the wording from this distance, but it's an orange logo of some sort, with black lettering. It's a temporary sign, designed to cover the actual logo beneath it. I've seen few vans with small logos painted on the front passenger side. Ropic Industries has one. And their vans are white, also.

I look around to see if anyone's behind me. I want to check on the lady, but the little voice in my head says, *Why? To ask if she's okay?*

Then it adds, *You're alone, miles from your safe place. What if the van circles behind you?*

I look at the office and industrial buildings around me, and decide to go vertical.

Running down the alley between two buildings, I spot a staircase, and take it up to the second floor landing. There's a flat roof ten feet above me. I stand on the railing and carefully raise my arms over my head, grab the roof ledge and pull myself up to about chest height. I swing my right leg up and hook my foot over the ledge and work my way onto the roof. From there, I get a running start and jump to the next roof, then the next, and soon I'm on the rooftop of a building, looking down at the intersection where the white van had been moments earlier.

I lay flat on the roof and wait to see if anyone comes to check on the body.

While I'm doing that, the building beneath me explodes.

2.

AS I JUMP to my feet to survey the damage below, I quickly conclude the building beneath me is collateral damage. Based on my knowledge of where the woman had been sitting moments earlier, and seeing only the remnants of her ass there now, it's clear she'd been wired with explosives.

Which makes her a homeland terrorist.

I press the button that speed-dials Callie.

"Where are you?" she says.

"Corner of Landmark and Trace. Heading north on Landmark, right side of the street. Make it fast!"

"Give me two minutes."

I hang up, check the street below me, and notice several structures have been decimated.

But why?

I mean, why here? Why now? Nothing in the immediate area remotely resembles a terrorist target.

I'd love to investigate the scene, try to work it out, but within minutes the cops will be swarming the area, and I need to be long gone by then. Whatever role the driver of the white van played in all this, I doubt he's planning to hang around to deal with me. I carefully work my way down the back side of the building, thankful the blast hasn't done too much damage.

A couple minutes later I'm in the passenger side of Callie's black Mercedes CL65 AMG.

"Sweet car," I say.

"You're not bleeding, right?" she says.

"Not that I know of."

She turns right, makes the block, begins heading back to her place. Says, "If I knew you were this filthy, I'd have stolen a car."

"Sorry. I was lying on something nasty just now."

"You really need to upgrade your taste in women."

"I was talking about a nasty rooftop."

"Still."

I sigh. "There *was* a woman, though."

"Of course there was," Callie says. Then adds, "What happened to her?"

"You know how some people in Vegas lose their heads, and some lose their asses?"

"Yeah?"

"She lost both."

3.

I'M IN CALLIE'S penthouse condo now. The lovely Gwen has changed her hair to platinum blond, and it's working for her. She sees me and races toward me, as if she's about to give me a big hug. But as she gets close, she stops short and wrinkles her nose.

"You smell," she says.

"I know." To Callie I say, "Can I shower in your guest bedroom?"

"Of course," she says.

I enter the guest bedroom and pause to look at a group of items lined up on the dresser.

"What's all this?" I call to Callie.

"Oops," she says from the living room. Then adds, "When you called, Gwen and I were about to have a sex marathon. We set some things out we planned to use."

"Really?" I say.

She and Gwen enter the room.

The three of us look at the items on the dresser. There's a scarf, a vibrator, lipstick, a deck of cards, a condom, three bullets, and a bird cage.

Callie gives Gwen a look I can't decipher.

Gwen shrugs.

I study the items another minute, then say. "It makes sense."

Callie says, "It does?"

"Except for one item," I say.

Callie laughs. "The birdcage?"

"Nope."

She looks surprised. "No? Then what?"

"The condom."

Callie frowns at Gwen, then says, "But you understand the birdcage."

"I do."

"And the bullets?" she says.

"What about them?"

"They make sense to you?"

"Of course."

"But not the condom."

"Not the condom."

She shrugs, looks at Gwen again. Says, "He doesn't understand the condom."

Gwen says, "Go figure."

I look at the items again.

"Ah!" I say.

"Ah?"

"The condom goes on the vibrator!"

They look at each other.

"Go take your shower," Callie says.

4.

Two Weeks Earlier...

MAYBE TAYLOR CROSSES the street and enters the park without attracting attention. No surprise there, she rarely attracts attention, though she's above average cute. Her body has slimmed down this year, thanks to her strict diet and four-hour-a-day exercise regimen. Still, if she's being honest—and she usually is—a couple pounds of teenage belly fat continues to cling to her five-five frame as tenaciously as puke on a drunk's beard.

Maybe entered the world a natural blond, but age has darkened her hair to the point that now, at age twenty, it matches *mission brown* on the wood stain color chart at Harvey's Hardware, Jacksonville, Florida.

Maybe wants to be prettier, but lacks the angular face and high cheekbones common to classic beauties. Her eyes are nice, she always gets compliments on those. People seem to be drawn to blue-eyed girls, even when there's nothing else particularly special about them. Maybe's breasts would be picture perfect...if they didn't fan out in opposite directions. But they do, and it embarrasses her when boys do a double-take, like they weren't expecting her nipples to be practically under her arm pits. No one looks better in a bra than Maybe.

But when the bra comes off, the breasts fly wide right and left, like a field goal kicker with the yips.

Like the rest of Maybe's physical package, things could be much worse. A flat chest, for example, would be ten times worse. Still, there's no single feature she's exceptionally proud of.

Wait...

Her ass is nice.

She wouldn't change her ass. Not that she goes out of her way to stare at it, but it *must* be pretty special, or the boys who've seen it wouldn't make such a fuss. Not that she's shown it to many boys.

She hasn't.

Anyway, it's not Maybe's ass that's caused her problems. It's the other private place. And that part has had a *huge* effect on her. How huge? It's basically turned her into a mental patient.

Maybe walks to the area of the park where giant rocks protrude from a hill, and climbs to a spot from which she can see all around her. When she's confident no one can hear her conversation, she presses a button on her phone. When the man answers, she says, "Hi Daddy, it's Maybe."

"Hi, honey," he says.

She pauses a moment, then says, "You stopped disguising your voice!"

"Do you like my real voice?"

"Yes! Thank you! But it's been a year. Why now?"

"Isn't it obvious?"

"Not so much."

"I've fallen in love with you."

Maybe pauses a minute to process this revelation. Then says, "I've been bad, Daddy."

"Tell me."

"I kissed a boy."

The man on the other end of the phone pauses.

She adds, "I kissed a boy and I liked it."

Maybe smiles, knowing he understands what she's really done.

The man says, "Where is he now?"

"His place."

"Did you leave any evidence?"

"Of course not, Daddy."

"How did you meet him?"

"In the parking lot outside a sports bar."

"Any cameras?"

"No."

"How'd you get to his place?"

"I drove."

"Where'd you leave your car?"

"I drove to a shopping center two miles from his house. Then I got my bike out of the trunk, attached the front tire to it, and rode it to his place. When I got close, I called and told him to open his garage door. When he did, I rode right in. Then he closed the door. You'll be so proud of me!"

"Tell me why."

"I wore a ball cap and put my hair in a pony tail. Put an extra shirt in my bike pack. Didn't eat anything, or drink anything, and didn't even go inside the house."

"Did you let him touch you?"

"Just my boobs. He pushed me back against his car and started messing around and when he started trying to pull my pants down I reached in the back pocket, took the syringe, and stuck him."

"And you pushed the poison into him?"

12

"Yup. At first his head went straight up, and his chin looked like it was going to hit the ceiling! He knocked my hand off the syringe, but the poison was already in him. He couldn't reach the syringe, so I stepped out of the way and watched him dance."

"Which way did he fall?"

Maybe frowns. "You don't believe me."

"Of course I do."

She pauses, then says, "He fell forward, face first, onto his car."

"And was he dead?"

"Not yet. His legs shook awhile, and he couldn't get a full breath. Then he couldn't get a half breath. Then he couldn't get a breath at all."

The man pauses before saying, "Did you happen to take a souvenir?"

"Of course not, Daddy! What, do you think I'm stupid?"

"You're far from stupid, Baby."

"Call me Maybe."

He sighs. "I don't like the name you've chosen, and I don't like what it represents."

"Until I decide how far I'm willing to go, I'm Maybe."

"I understand that. But I don't like it."

"But you like *me*, don't you, Daddy?"

"I love you."

"Thank you, Daddy."

"I love you deeply," he says.

"I'm glad."

"And you?"

"What?" Maybe asks.

"Do you love me?"

"No."

He remains quiet, obviously disappointed.

Then Maybe says, "But I *want* to."

She tries to imagine the expression on his face, but has nothing to go on but the sound of his voice. After a few moments he says, "How are things going with Dr. Scott?"

"I don't want to talk about that. It's embarrassing."

"You can tell me anything. You know that, right?"

"You already know. You're the one who's paying him to see me. You probably get updates after each visit."

"It's not the same as asking you about it."

"I don't like to talk about it."

He pauses again. "I understand. So. Are you ready for a *real* assignment?"

Maybe's face lights up. "Yes! Absolutely!"

"I want you to…kiss…a college professor. Can you do that?"

"Of course, Daddy."

5.

Present Day...
Donovan Creed.

"WHEN YOU SAY she lost her head," Callie says, "what do you mean?"

I shrug. "The top and sides of her head exploded."

"Where was the bomb? In her mouth?"

"Inside her head."

"What?"

"It had to be a very small explosive, either on top of her head, or inside her skull. Hard as it is to imagine, I think it was inside."

"Like your brain chip?"

"Except that it explodes instead of heating up," I say.

"Lucky's company?"

"It's possible."

Jim "Lucky" Peters, the famous Vegas gambler, was murdered one week ago. As it happens, Callie's lover, Eva LeSage, was murdered at the same time. Callie's *current* love interest, Gwen, is Lucky's widow.

Small world, right?

Twenty feet from us, in Callie's kitchen, Gwen's eating a bowl of Lucky Charms, oblivious to the irony. She's wearing boxer shorts and a scarlet UNLV T-shirt with gray lettering.

Gwen isn't *Callie hot*, but you could fry an egg on any part of her.

Callie sees me staring at her girlfriend.

"Down, boy," she says.

"I saw her first," I say.

It's true. I seduced Gwen hours before Callie met her.

"But I saw her best," Callie says.

Also true. While I've never had complaints from the women I've dated, Callie has a double advantage over me. First, she and Gwen share the same plumbing. Second, she understands the handbook, meaning she can make sense out of all the emotional wiring a woman brings into the bedroom. All the unspoken stuff Callie instinctively understands allows her to not only be Gwen's physical partner, but her emotional tampon, as well.

Gwen was bisexual when I met her, so Callie didn't *turn* her. But Callie won her away from me in record time.

It wasn't even a contest.

There are other reasons. The fact I already have a steady girlfriend, Rachel, may have been a factor. Also, Callie's a drop-dead gorgeous force of nature, and fiercely monogamous, while I have a tendency to stray. I mean, I don't lie about it. I just haven't found the right woman yet. Well, that's not entirely true. I found the right woman at least twice. But that's a story for the second bourbon. Also, Callie lives in a multi-million dollar penthouse condo and I often live in the attics of strangers. Gwen probably feels more secure with Callie. She just lost her husband, Callie just lost her girlfriend, and Lucky's estate is in Vegas. Callie lives in Vegas. Makes sense, right?

Here's how things got to this point: Lucky and Gwen were having a weekly three-way with Callie's girlfriend. When

Callie caught Lucky and Eva fucking, she killed them on the spot, but spared Gwen for my benefit. Fate brought Gwen and Callie together, then they connected, and they've been together ever since.

Meaning two whole weeks.

I'm still holding out hope that Gwen realizes there's something missing in her relationship with Callie.

A penis.

Something I've got in abundance.

Well, something I've got, anyway.

Gwen's got something, too. Behind one of her implants, she's hiding a small, ceramic device that can be programmed to kill me. It's…

Look, it's a long story.

I've got a chip in my brain. Not the kind that blows up like the lamp post lady's did this morning, but the kind that turns white-hot and can liquefy my brain. My version is less messy than hers, but just as lethal. And while her chip appears to have been activated from a van, close by, I assume it works like the chip in my brain, which can be activated by satellite from nearly anywhere in the world. I don't know if our chips are related, but I have to assume they are. What I do know is the device Gwen has behind her boob can kill me. And I aim to have it.

Other than the fact I'd like to spend some horizontal time with Gwen, I'm hanging around Vegas till I can retrieve the device from behind Gwen's boob.

Sounds ridiculous, right? But what're you going to do?

It is what it is.

Callie and I have explained all this to Gwen, but she's reluctant to do the surgery. If it weren't for Callie, I'd perform the surgery myself. But Gwen's boobs are spectacular, even better than her husband, Lucky's, boob job had been. Lucky had gotten his boobs after losing a bet, and...

Never mind.

I know what you're thinking. This whole situation is nuts. Well, it's even nuttier than you think: Lucky's girlfriend was the plastic surgeon who performed Gwen's implant surgery.

But still. Her boobs are like the eighth wonder of the world, and you'd hate to mess that up. Nevertheless, I can't allow Gwen's boobs to fall into the wrong hands.

It could literally be the end of me.

So I'm losing my patience.

"I'll give you till three o'clock to set the appointment," I say to Callie. "Otherwise, I'm going to take matters into my own hands."

"Don't threaten me," Callie says.

Callie's my protégé. Aside from me, she's the deadliest human on the planet. I could be wrong about us being the two deadliest. After all, I haven't met *every* human on the planet. But I'm in the killing business, so I know most of the deadly ones, and so far we're one and two on the list. A formidable combination, we are, and based on a great working relationship, one I'd like to maintain.

Which means I'm not going to let a pair of boobs come between us. On the other hand, I aim to have that chip. Callie knows this. She may have a thing for Gwen, but she needs me more. We're government assassins, and I'm the key to her job opportunities. There are six of us. I run the crew, Callie's my main operative. So she'll come through. I'm waiting for her to say something right now about it. She's about to say something.

But doesn't.

"I mean it," I say.

And I do. I stand.

"Where are you going?" Callie says.

"To visit Ropic Industries."

"You'll never get in the door."

I smile. Callie doesn't know I've been planning this for a full week. Gwen doesn't know, either.

Callie frowns. "What're you up to?"

I nod my chin toward the kitchen, indicating Gwen. "When Lucky died, Gwen became the majority stockholder of Ropic Industries," I say.

"So?"

I let her think about that for a minute. Then a smile slowly spreads across Callie's face.

It's a helluva face.

6.

BETWEEN SWALLOWS OF Lucky Charms, Gwen asks what she has to do.

"Show up with me at an emergency meeting of the board," I say.

She loads a spoon with cereal, puts it in her mouth, chews, and swallows it.

"Most people take milk in their cereal," I say.

"Most people aren't me," Gwen says.

Callie and I exchange a look that ends with Callie smiling from out of Gwen's field of vision. It crosses my mind that if I tell Gwen Callie's laughing at her behind her back, I might be able to gain the advantage in the quest for Gwen's considerable charms. But I quickly dismiss the thought. Not because I'm above such deviousness, but because I need the two of them on my side today.

Gwen pushes some cereal around in her bowl with her index finger, separates a rainbow candy piece from the rest, and balances it on her perfect nose. "Watch this," she says, turning her head sideways so Callie can also see. She drops her chin and catches the rainbow on her tongue, moves her tongue in and out of her mouth more seductively than it sounds, then swallows the rainbow. Then she shows us a goofy smile.

"The trick is to let it slide off your nose slowly," she says, as gravely as if explaining how to disarm a land mine. "Most people drop their chin too fast."

Though Callie and I both nod thoughtfully, I doubt "most" people have ever given a thought to balancing cereal on their noses.

Here's the skinny on Gwen: she was the child bride of Lucky Peters. He saved her from a life of stripping in mob-controlled clubs, gave her a nice home and an air of respectability. But Lucky's good fortune deserted him, and their life together went downhill fast. I doubt Gwen ever loved him. As far as I can tell, she doesn't even *miss* him. Not only did she have sex with *me* hours before Lucky was killed, she had sex with Callie hours *after* he was killed!

So, yes, Gwen and I shared an intimate afternoon. Our first session was tepid at best. But then I discovered she's a power whore. Meaning, power makes her horny. And the more powerful she perceives you to be, the wilder she gets.

It's something to see.

And feel.

She's a beautiful, sensual woman. Not in Callie's league, as I've said, but a solid ten, nevertheless.

When she's not crunching Lucky Charms.

"I don't know how to conduct a board meeting," she says.

"I'll run the meeting as your advisor, but don't worry. They'll know you're in charge."

"Your presence at the meeting will only convince them *you're* in charge," Gwen says.

Callie and I exchange a look that ends with Callie lifting an eyebrow as if to say, *she's smarter than she appears*.

And she is.

You don't want to underestimate Gwen just because strange comments occasionally escape her cereal-stained mouth.

7.

WE'RE IN THE car. Gwen's wearing the single most seductive dress I've ever seen. It's an open-shouldered silk and satin blend that drapes in the front all the way to her navel! The color is an intense, in-your-face red, and the dress is obscenely short. A good ten inches above her knees *before* she sat in the car, which means there's a lot of thigh riding in the passenger seat of my rental. Even from my angle I can see that Gwen has managed to perfectly match her panties to her dress, which has long been her fashion hallmark.

"Gwen."

She turns toward me.

"How would you describe the color of your dress?"

She looks at me like I'm a moron, then speaks slowly, as if talking to a foreign child who barely understands English. "In our country, we call this color red."

"Funny. I'm actually wondering about the shade of red."

"What about it?"

"Is there a name for it?"

"Thinking of buying one for your girlfriend?"

I frown.

"It's called the new red," she says.

I take another peek. "It's a hell of a dress! The most outrageous one I've ever seen."

"The dress is up here. Follow the sound of my voice."

Bottom line, it's a shockingly short, kick-ass red dress, and she's wearing it well.

"You think the board members will approve?"

"If they don't, I'll shoot them."

Without actually saying so, I've led Callie and Gwen to believe I'm driving Gwen to Ropic Industries. In reality I'm driving her to PhySpa, the plastic surgery center and spa that used to belong to Ropic's former medical director, Dr. Phyllis Willis. After Phyllis and half her staff were found brutally murdered, I managed to purchase PhySpa for pennies on the dollar. Though local police have kept the crime scene tape in place, I happen to know they've concluded their investigation, and doubt they'll be back. With their permission, I hired a half-dozen security personnel to keep an eye on things until the cops officially release the premises to me. They guard the outside of the building, and were only allowed inside on one occasion, and that was to help the delivery guys carry the two large freezers I ordered to be placed in the spa.

Why do I need freezers in the spa?

That's another story for another time.

In a month I intend to re-open the surgical center and spa, under the direction of Dr. Eamon Petrovsky, who headed the team of surgeons that reconstructed my face a couple years ago. I plan to call it Vegas Moon, if that meets with Gwen's approval.

How did I get the board members to agree to a secret meeting at PhySpa? I told them Gwen Peters was ready to discuss her role with the company, now that her husband was dead. I told them she was considering two possibilities: accepting a cheap buyout for her controlling interest, or using her inheritance to make a major investment in Ropic Industries. Knowing either event would stimulate their greed glands, I explained the meeting should be held in secret, away from their headquarters. I told them my driver, Jeff Tuck, would pick them up in a nearby restaurant parking lot and bring them here.

Of course, they probably felt funny ducking under the crime scene tape and entering the back door, just as Gwen and I are doing now.

Jeff Tuck holds the door for us, and we enter. I nod at Joe Penny, who's standing just inside. Jeff's my eccentric L.A. operative, and Joe Penny's the young bomb-builder and computer whiz I hired to upgrade the surveillance system and wire the building. Thanks to Joe Penny and my unlimited budget, PhySpa is a veritable fortress. I know, because I've been living here quietly since two days after I killed Dr. Phyllis Willis.

"Is Dr. P. here?" I say.

Jeff's eyes start to tear up. "You're so beautiful!" he says.

"Thanks," I say.

"Her," he says.

"Thank you," Gwen says. Then smiles and adds, "I'm Gwen."

Jeff looks her up and down. "You certainly are." He looks at me. "How do you do it?"

"Let's move along."

Young Joe Penny is so stupefied by Gwen's legs I leave him there to recover.

I don't blame the guys. Gwen is spectacular. Still…

"Jeff," I say.

"Yeah?"

"Try to be professional."

Jeff nods, and escorts Gwen and me down a short hallway.

"That wasn't here before," Gwen says, indicating the small

24

glass-walled cubicle that's blocking our way.

"It's for security," I say. "Watch what I do, then do the same."

I enter the cubicle, and Jeff closes the door behind me. I place my feet on the two small dots on the concrete floor, put my hands on the glass walls on either side of the cubicle, and close my eyes. Five seconds later a beep sounds, and I exit through the opposite door, close it, and wait for Gwen to enter the cubicle. She does, but turns sideways while looking for the dot upon which to place her right foot. Without meaning to, she strikes one of the sexiest poses I've ever seen! Her hip is practically touching one side of the cubicle, and her left foot, the other. She's wearing five-inch black stilettos with a single black ankle strap. Of course, at this angle, the front of her dress is almost completely open.

Just as I'm wishing I had a picture of her in this pose, Jeff snaps one with his cell phone. I'll confiscate it later. Eventually Gwen gets her feet situated properly, waits for the beep, then joins me on the other side of the cubicle, and together we wait for Jeff.

He joins us and we continue down the hall to the surgery center, where Gwen and I visit with the brilliant Dr. P. for a few minutes. I own the building, but I'm giving Dr. P. eighty percent of the actual business to run the place. He'll bring class and credibility to the plastic surgery center, and will soon conduct interviews to hire a manager to run the spa.

We can't use the former spa manager because I killed him the morning I shot Phyllis.

As we head to the spa's consultation room, Gwen says, "You *bought* this place?"

"I did."

"I had no idea you were rich."

25

What she means is she assumed I took the job as Lucky's bodyguard because I needed the cash. Being obscenely wealthy would normally be enough to win Gwen. In fact, the *only* thing Lucky had going for him when he met her was his fifty million dollar financial statement. By the time I met him, six months later, Lucky was flat broke. Even his controlling interest in Ropic Industries was worthless, since the company's stock had been de-listed.

Gwen puts her hand on my arm to stop me. Jeff Tuck tenses up, just like I taught him, ready to strike, should there be a problem. I nod to let him know I'm okay.

"I like a man with money!" Gwen coos.

Of course she does. But Callie's wealthy too, weighing in with a billion dollar net worth statement. The fact I'm six times wealthier than Callie merely keeps me in the game.

Gwen stands on her tiptoes and kisses my earlobe.

"Have you missed me?" she says.

"I have."

"Why?"

"Excuse me?"

"I mean, why did you buy PhySpa?"

The way she changes subjects reminds me of my girlfriend, Rachel, who I'm allowed to call once a week. Thinking about it now, I realize it's been a week since my last call.

"I didn't care about the spa part," I say. "But a plastic surgery center in Vegas? Where every woman wants boobs and the best plastic surgeon in the world is available to run the place? It's a no-brainer!"

She purses her lips and says, "I think about you all the time."

I suspect she's only thought about me since discovering I might be wealthy a moment ago. But no matter. Gwen's desire to be around rich, powerful people notwithstanding, it dawns on me she's as easy-going as any woman could be. She was glad to sit in Callie's kitchen munching dry cereal, being left out of my conversation with Callie, and just as happy to attend a board meeting she knows nothing about. She didn't ask why I brought her to PhySpa instead of Ropic Industries, and I doubt she cares. She didn't complain about entering the security cubicle, nor when we took time to visit Dr. P.

THERE ARE SIX people in the consultation room of PhySpa when Gwen and I enter, all of whom are giving off a bored, who-gives-a-shit attitude. A middle-aged guy with thick glasses and no eyebrows sits at the head of the long table. He's William Wadsworth, the CEO. I know, because I've done my homework. I spent the past week reading everything about Ropic Industries my facilitator, Lou Kelly, has dug up on the company since the day I met Lucky Peters. Plus, I have insider information I gleaned from Lucky prior to his death.

William clears his throat to speak, but I put a stop to that by slamming my fist on the table and shouting, "Get your ass out of the chair, William, 'cause there's a new sheriff in town!"

He grimaces at my lack of couth, but remains where he's sitting. I grab my gun from my ankle holster and point it at him.

He tries to lower his head into his suit coat, turtle-like, while raising his hands. I notice the others have snapped to attention.

"Put your hands down," I say. "This isn't a robbery, it's a hostile takeover."

He scrambles out of the chair, and Gwen sits in it, smiles brightly, and says, "Why, *thank* you, William!" Then she points at my gun and says, "I thought we just went through security."

"We did," I say, "but I own the joint."

"Ah," she says.

I say, "Put your cell phones on the table, everyone."

Tony Spumoni, Ropic's president, says, "Cell phones aren't allowed at board meetings."

I point my gun at his face. "Cell phones on the table."

Everyone places their cell phones in the center of the table.

I retrieve mine from my jacket, and press a button. When Joe Penny answers, I ask him to join us.

Seconds later, Joe enters. I tell him to collect the phones. While we're in the meeting, he'll download their recent calls and text messages so I can see what they've been up to. He gathers the phones and leaves, as I announce, "I'm Donovan Creed, Mrs. Peters's advisor. Anyone have a problem with my being here?"

No one says anything.

"Good." I holster my weapon. "Which of you ladies is Mary?"

Mary tentatively raises her hand a few inches.

"You're the corporate secretary?"

She nods.

"What have you written down so far?"

"N-nothing."

"Good. Let's keep it that way. I'll provide the minutes later, and you can sign them."

"Th-that's not normally how it's d-done," she says.

"Right. And the way you people run a company isn't the way it's normally done, either."

"What are you insinuating?" William says.

"Ropic Industries is under federal investigation for accounting irregularities."

"Thanks to her husband!" Tony says, with contempt.

"That's a rather nasty tone to take, under the circumstances," I say. "Can't you see Mrs. Peters is grieving over the loss of her husband?"

Everyone takes a minute to look at Gwen, but no, they can't detect any sadness in her face. I ask, "Which of you is Stevie, the accountant?"

"Stephen Derrier is no longer with us," William says.

"He's dead?"

"He's been relieved of his duties, awaiting federal investigation for misappropriation of corporate funds."

"Why's that a federal offense?"

"He and Lucky Peters conspired to fund a casino wagering scheme."

I arch an eyebrow.

"That's right, Mr. Creed," William says, smugly. "We turned ourselves in to the authorities, pled our case, and they're giving us an opportunity to stay in business."

"Only in Vegas," I say.

"That's right. And you should know that since Mrs. Peters's husband was directly involved in the embezzlement of more than $12 million of corporate assets, our attorneys are working to divest her of his shares and redistribute them to the shareholders."

I look around the table and see they're all wearing smug smiles. They think I'm losing control of the meeting.

They're wrong.

I say, "Since Ropic has no in-house attorneys, you must have hired outside counsel."

"That's right."

"How much was their retainer?"

William smiles. "That's really none of your business."

"Is it safe to say you paid more than fifty thousand

dollars?"

"We're a public company. You can learn those specifics at the next shareholder meeting, should you care to attend."

"Assuming you're a registered stock holder," Toni Spumoni adds, with a sneer.

I walk to the door, open it, and Jeff Tuck enters, closes the door behind him, and plants himself in front of it. I remove my jacket, then grab the neck of the board member sitting closest to the door, and lift him out of his chair while applying enough pressure to make him wet his pants, violently.

"Now, see *here*!" William says, rising to his feet.

"I don't feel like waiting till the next shareholder meeting," I say. "Who's this guy with the weak bladder?"

"Mr. Shay."

"And he's?"

"Our new accountant."

I notice Gwen's face getting flushed, which doesn't mean she's embarrassed. Quite the contrary, it means she's getting turned on by my display of power.

I look at the lady sitting beside Mr. Shay. She's cowering, trying to avoid eye contact. "And who's this?" I say.

No one speaks, but I already know she's Tootie Greene, Ropic's executive vice president.

I drop the urine-soaked accountant back in his chair and say, "Mrs. Greene? You can either tell me how much the company paid for outside legal counsel, or I can squeeze some piss out of you, too."

"Too late," she says.

A quick glance at the crotch of her tan slacks confirms she's telling the truth. From her place at the head of the table, Gwen exclaims, "Oh! Oh, *my*!"

Everyone looks at her, and she says, "Sorry."

But I can see she's positively smoldering. I wink at her, and she swallows hard. She fixes her gaze on me, waiting to see what I'm going to do next, clearly hoping I'll put on a show of power.

Tony says, "Fuck this. We paid 'em two hundred fifty grand. What're you gonna do about it?"

I smile and say, "The payment of funds in excess of fifty thousand dollars to any outside legal counsel requires a majority vote of the stockholders."

"Who says?"

I point to the stack of corporate documents by the house phone on the table hugging the far wall. "It's all in there. You should read your own rules sometime, Spumoni. At any rate, since Gwen's the majority stockholder of the company, your actions in hiring the outside firm constitute a breach of corporate policy. Mrs. Peters could fire you right now, if she cares to. Mrs. Peters?"

"Yes, Mr. Creed?"

"Do you approve spending two hundred fifty thousand dollars of corporate money to divest you of your shares?"

"What's that mean?"

"Do you want to let them take your company away from you?"

"Hell, no!"

"There's your mandate," I say, pointing to the house phone. "Tony, call the attorneys and fire them. Tell them to return any unused portion of the retainer."

"I'll do no such thing."

I start moving toward him.

"You can't intimidate me," he says, jumping to his feet. He takes up a boxing stance. I let him throw a punch at me. It's a roundhouse right that takes so long to arrive I almost fall asleep waiting for it. At the last second I duck under his punch, reach up, and tear off one of his ears.

9.

MARY SCREAMS. MRS. Greene vomits. Tony shrieks and runs to the corner of the room, and cowers, clutching the side of his head. Gwen's eyes roll up in her head. She gasps. Then swoons.

I look at the sixth man in the room. "Who're you?"

"George Best."

"VP, research and development?"

"Yes."

"I'll have some questions for you in a few minutes."

I toss Tony his ear and say, "Stop being a baby. Jeff, will you escort Mr. Spumoni to Dr. P.'s office? He'll have that ear back on by the time we adjourn."

Jeff helps Tony to his feet.

"This isn't over, Creed!" Tony shouts. "You're a dead man! Do you hear me? A dead man!"

"Yeah, I hear you," I say. "I've got two good ears."

"Asshole!" he shouts. "I won't rest till I kill you!"

"You can show me how tough you are when Gwen takes control of your company and sticks you in the mail room."

Gwen gasps, "Oh! Oh! OH!"

Everyone's looking at Gwen, including Jeff and Tony. Being a guy who knows an opportunity when he sees one, I spring into action. "Jeff, take Tony to Dr. P.'s office and guard him. Close the door behind you. Tell Joe to stay in his office. Mrs.

Peters and I need to confer in the hallway." To Gwen I say, "Mrs. Peters? Will you join me in the hallway to discuss this recent development?"

She jumps to her feet.

I could easily unplug the phone from the wall and take it with me, but where's the style in that? I grab the phone, rip it out of the wall, and fling it across the room. Gwen gasps, "Oh, Oh, OH!"

To the board members I say, "Stay put."

William says, "And if we don't?"

"I'll kill you."

Gwen shouts, "Oh, Oh, OH, OH My *God*! OH, OH, *OH MY GOD*!"

She and I race out of the room. I slam the door behind us and pin her against it, rip her panties off and take her right there in the hallway. Gwen moans and yelps and gasps as I give her all I've got. She pulls me into her again and again, and each time she does, her back slams against the door, making a loud banging sound. But that's nothing compared to the ear-splitting volume of her demonic shrieks and wolf-like howls.

The last time we power fucked was the best sex of my life, so I naturally assumed that had been her "A" game. But no. Today she's elevated her sexual frenzy to a level that transcends space and time! The combination of Gwen realizing I'm rich, and my sudden display of violence, and her growing awareness of her power in the company, and the fact that a roomful of important people are being forced to wait while we have sex right outside the door—has driven her over the edge.

It doesn't take me long to hit a nice stopping point, but Gwen's insatiable. We drop to the floor and I quickly realize this party has barely started.

I won't tell you what transpired next, or how long it lasted.

As for the commotion we raised, let's just say it was considerable. When Gwen and I re-enter the urine and vomit-infested room, her face is drained of all color and our knees are shaking. All eyes in the room turn to Gwen as she reclaims her place at the conference table while displaying not the least hint of embarrassment.

What a woman!

"Thanks for your patience," I tell the board members. "Mrs. Peters and I were engaged in a rather heated debate, and had to get something straight between us. I'm happy to report we achieved that goal."

"A *debate*?" Chairman Wadsworth says.

I give him a stern look and say, "Yes, of course. What did you think was going on?"

"Honestly? I thought a construction crew was demolishing the building."

I look around the table. "Anyone else?"

Tootie Greene raises her hand.

"Yes?"

"I thought someone was kicking the door while playing a high volume recording of killer whales singing across the ocean."

I look at Mary.

"Sir?"

"Anything to add?"

"To me it sounded like you were flogging an angry banshee. No offense, Mrs. Peters."

10.

"I'M AWARE THE conditions aren't ideal in here," I say, "but believe me, I've seen worse."

I call Joe Penny to fix the phone. While he does that, I coerce William into calling the attorneys. As he fires them, we learn they've already blown through half the contingency fee.

"You've wasted over a hundred grand," I say. "Now stop this nonsense, and I'll tell you why it wouldn't have worked in the first place. Your medical director, Dr. Phyllis Willis, was murdered in this very building two weeks ago, along with several members of her staff. What you may not know is *why*. Shall I tell you?"

No one speaks, so I continue.

"Dr. Willis helped supervise the implanting of a chip into the brain of a government assassin named Connor Payne. The chip can be activated by remote control. When a four-digit code is entered, the chip heats up and Mr. Payne's brains will liquefy. How many of you knew that, raise your hands."

No one does.

"George?" I say.

George reluctantly raises his hand. The others appear shocked.

"Your company, Ropic Industries, manufactured the chip."

"That's ridiculous!" William Wadsworth says.

"Tell them, George."

"You know it's true, William," George says. "You signed off on it."

Mary's jaw drops. She looks at William like he's a child molester.

"There's more. Phyllis was having an affair with Gwen's husband. When she performed Gwen's breast augmentation..." I pause so they can all take a moment to check out Gwen's boobs. They do, and continue staring at them until she finally crosses her arms over her chest. Then I say, "Phyllis placed a small ceramic device behind one of Gwen's implants. This device can kill Connor Payne, and he knows it. Which puts Gwen's life in danger, which means if she files a lawsuit, you're out of business."

I press a button on my cell phone. When Jeff answers, I ask, "How's the patient?"

"Sleeping."

"Tie him down and bring me Gwen's body scan."

Moments later I hold up the body scan we took of Gwen when she entered the security cubicle. Sure enough, behind her right boob, the device is visible.

"Hey!" Gwen says. "That was a dirty trick, telling me I was going through security."

I shrug. "It gets worse. This morning a bomb went off on Trace Street."

"That's common knowledge," George says.

"It's all you see on the news," William adds. "Apparently a suicide bomber was heading toward the convention center when her vest exploded."

"*Her* vest?" I say. "I don't recall the police releasing that information."

William looks down. Mary walks over to him and stands there until he looks up. When he does, she slaps his face.

38

"We're through!" she says, and makes a move for the door. I wonder if anyone knew before today that William and Mary were having an affair.

I put my arm out to stop her, and say, "Stay put, Mary. We're all family here. This room may not be soundproof…"

I wink at Gwen.

She gives me the finger.

"…But it's safe for conversations."

Mary reclaims her seat.

"You folks have been breaking the law," I say. "You're dealing with terrorists."

"That's ridiculous," William says.

"You're selling chips that can be detonated by remote control. The woman on Trace Street walked into a lamp post, fell on her ass, and her head blew up. Tell me that's not an explosive chip manufactured by your company that was placed in her brain."

I give George a hard look and start moving toward him.

He says, "The chip was sewn into her mouth."

Everyone turns to look at George. He says, "These chips are like blasting caps. We manufactured hundreds of them for the government, but they canceled the contract. I sold them to an arms dealer for two million dollars."

"What was the government planning to use them for?"

"I have no idea."

"How do you know the device was in her mouth?"

"The arms dealer called me to complain about the size of the explosion."

"What do you mean?"

"I may have given them the impression the chips could take down a building."

"They would have demanded a test."

"We blew up a car."

"How's that possible?"

"The test was rigged."

"You're joking."

"I tossed a chip into a car and detonated it. But the seats were filled with plastic explosives."

"You're dumb enough to cheat an arms dealer?"

"We were desperate. Our company was about to go broke. We needed the cash infusion."

"Why was the woman's chest wired with explosives?"

"They were testing the chip, but wanted a backup to destroy the evidence in case it didn't work. They picked an illegal alien, threatened to kill her children, sewed the chip in her mouth, and sent her for a walk. When she got to Trace Street, she was crying so hard she walked into a post and fell down. She refused to get up, so they detonated the chip, surveyed the damage, and blew up the evidence. If this information goes public, we'll all wind up in prison."

William says, "We didn't intend the chips to be used by terrorists. But it happened, and now you know. So what is it you want?"

"I want Gwen on the board and her shares reinstated."

"That's preposterous!" William says, "It's common knowledge Mrs. Peters is a former stripper. The stockholders would never approve such a move."

"You think they'd rather be represented by terrorist sympathizers?"

He sighs. "What else do you want?"

I look at Gwen. "If you could run any kind of business in the world, what would it be?"

She thinks a moment. Then says, "I'd like to design and sell T-shirts."

"There you have it," I say. "Gwen's going to introduce a line of T-shirts."

"You're insane!" William says.

"You think she could possibly piss away more money with a T-shirt venture than you've lost with your business plan?"

"That's not the point. We're not in clothing. We're an electronics company."

"How about electronic T-shirts?" Gwen says.

"How about that!" I say, beaming at her. "She's already created a tie-in!"

Gwen beams back.

"I want something too," I say.

"Of course you do," William says. "What?"

"An introduction to your arms dealer."

"Why?"

"I'm going to eliminate this terror cell."

"I want something else," Gwen says. "An assistant. And maybe a private secretary!"

"Then you shall have one," I say. "Right, Mr. Wadsworth?"

"The inmates are running the asylum," he says.

11.

Ten Days Earlier...
Maybe Taylor.

"ARE YOU KIDDING me?"

"It's the next logical step," Dr. Scott says.

They're in the bookcase-lined office Dr. Scott uses for their intimate discussions. Maybe has no idea how many rooms are in Dr. Scott's building, but she's seen three, which is probably half of them. What she's never seen is a secretary or any other employee. That's because Dr. Scott stopped accepting new patients shortly after scheduling Maybe. Truth is, she was lucky to get in. Between the lobby and this room, Dr. Scott has a workspace where he handled all their early-stage interviews.

Maybe and Dr. Scott are clearly past that stage today.

She studies the tray of dildos arranged vertically on the cabinet beside her recliner. There are six in all, ranging from tiny to enormous. Each is a different color. The smallest is the length and shape of a tampon, but half the diameter. That one's yellow. Next size up is tampon-sized and light blue. Next is green, then pink, then red. The cucumber is purple. A small tube of sexual lubricant completes the display.

Maybe frowns.

Dr. Scott says, "What's going through your mind right now?"

"You don't want to know."

"I *need* to know. If we're to make progress here."

"What's going through my mind is I'm wondering if you really think I'm going to let you shove these disgusting things into me."

"I normally let the patient introduce the devices as it suits her."

"And what if it doesn't suit me at all?"

"That's always a matter of your choice. But as we've discussed—"

"I know what we've discussed. We've discussed it *endlessly*! And now that we've spent an hour a day for six weeks talking about the physical and mental implications of vaginismus, you've somehow come to the conclusion today's the day I'm supposed to spread my legs and give you a vertical smile?"

"It's not a matter of exposing yourself. It's a matter of taking the next logical step forward in your treatment."

"So now we enter phase two," Maybe says.

"If you wish to call it that, I won't quibble."

"I'd call it the rape phase."

Dr. Scott sighs. "Let's take a step back to consider the effect the mere presence of these devices is having on you."

"Yeah, let's do that," Maybe says. "What if I brought out the same tray and told you to shove them up your ass while I watch?"

"There would be no purpose served by that exercise."

Maybe stares at the purple dildo and comes to the conclusion it's actually larger than it first appeared, if such could be possible.

"You must treat farm animals," she says.

"What draws you to that conclusion?"

Maybe points to the tray. "Mr. Purple."

Dr. Scott follows her gaze. "Perhaps I should remind you how babies enter the world."

"Don't waste your breath. I can't get a *tampon* inside me, let alone a penis. So you can put Mr. Purple back in the sack with the rest of your baseball gear."

"Mr. Purple, as you call the device, is simply here to give you a visual perspective of what's possible. It also serves the purpose of showing you how small our goal is for today."

"And what *is* the goal for today?"

"We'll introduce the smallest device today, and introduce it repeatedly, until we're completely comfortable. Tomorrow we'll continue working with it. Eventually, we'll work our way up to the larger sizes."

"I notice you're saying 'we.'"

"Yes, of course. I'm your doctor. We're achieving this goal together."

"Your part sounds awfully damn easy."

"In what way?"

"You get paid two hundred dollars an hour to watch me play with myself."

Dr. Scott frowns.

Maybe says, "I assume you intend to watch?"

"As we've discussed numerous times, I'm not a voyeur. I need to observe what happens to you physically in order to judge your reaction emotionally. We don't have to do this today, if you'd rather not. But if not now, when?"

They go back and forth like this for ten minutes before Dr. Scott brings her two gowns.

"What's the second one for?" she asks.

"To place beneath you on the recliner."

"Do I have to take my top off?"

"No. I'll leave the room while you get undressed."

44

"Just turn your head."

He does.

As she disrobes from the waist down, she says, "This is bullshit."

"How so?"

"There's no benefit to the gown. The whole point is for you to stare at my vagina while I try to insert the yellow dildo."

Maybe first heard of vaginismus six months ago, when she finally sat down with her OBGYN for a heart-to-heart. It took her another six weeks to get up the courage to talk to a specialist about it. According to Dr. Scott, vaginismus is a reflex of the PC muscle that causes the vagina to suddenly tense, making any type of vaginal penetration painful or impossible. It's a condition that prevents Maybe from having any type of vaginal penetration, including inserting a tampon, receiving a gynecological exam, and of course, having sexual intercourse. Nothing enters the V.

Wasn't always that way.

That's what makes it so frustrating. Two years ago Maybe had no problems with this. She was able to use tampons, receive proper exams, enjoy sex a time or two—was in all respects going through life happy as a bearded clam. But then something happened. Something psychological, according to Maybe's OBGYN.

Dr. Scott spent six weeks testing that theory, during which time Maybe has made exactly *no* progress on her own while playing the home version of the game. Now it's time to test the physiological response in a clinical atmosphere. According to Dr. Scott, Maybe isn't shutting her vaginal doors on purpose. The vaginismic affect is similar to the way your eyes involuntarily close when you sneeze, or when an object comes flying toward them. The degree of pain varies from one patient to the next when penetration is attempted, but Maybe's pain is intolerable.

"You can turn around now," she tells him.

He turns and scoots his chair closer and takes a position directly in front of her.

Maybe says, "What, no table and stirrups?"

"In my experience, the recliner is comfortable, and far less clinical. Our objective is to improve your everyday life, not condition you solely to accept gynecological examinations."

Maybe takes a deep breath, closes her eyes, and slowly lifts her gown. She remains that way for half a minute, feeling the tears spilling from the corners of her eyes. She slowly separates her legs until her ankles are three feet apart. She opens her eyes and sees Dr. Scott staring at her private area.

Which causes her tears to flow twice as hard.

He hands her the yellow dildo.

"Do you have any idea how embarrassing this is for me?" Maybe says.

"I do." he says.

"*Do* you?"

12.

Present Day...
Donovan Creed.

"THIS BETTER BE good," Callie says, when I show her the device that had been resting comfortably behind Gwen's boob two hours ago.

Gwen doesn't look at me before speaking. We've already made a pact. She'll assume full responsibility for the surgery if I don't tell Callie what happened between us in the hallway.

"Donovan took me to meet Dr. P.," Gwen says, "and he did a scan."

"Dr. Pee?" Callie says, looking at me.

"Dr. Petrovsky," I say. "The surgeon who reconstructed my face."

She looks at Gwen. "And *that* didn't concern you?"

Gwen giggles. "Donovan is gorgeous. You've said so yourself!"

I look at Callie. "You said that?"

"She's delusional. Must be the pain meds." To Gwen she said, "I thought we had an understanding about the boob job."

"You said I needed to do it. You just told me not to let Donovan bully me into it. And he didn't. When Dr. P. saw the scan, he said it would only take ten minutes to remove."

47

"And aesthetically?"

She looks at me.

I shrug. "How would I know?"

She looks back at Gwen. "Show me."

"Well, there's a bandage, but Dr. P. said in twelve weeks you won't be able to tell the difference."

"Twelve weeks?"

Callie looks at me.

"The recovery is only two weeks," I say. "Gwen's referring to the scar."

"Under my boob," Gwen says. Then winks. "Don't worry, sugar snatch. It'll be fine."

"Sugar snatch?" I say.

Callie's eyes blaze. "I ought to kill you both."

"Why me?" I say.

"For going behind my back on this."

"Why her?"

"For her big, fucking mouth."

Gwen's face falls. "I'm sorry," Gwen says.

"You should be. I wouldn't repeat *anything* you say to me in private. Nor would I cheapen our relationship by revealing our pet names. You don't deserve me. Move into some attic with him, if that's all our relationship means to you."

Gwen starts crying.

Callie watches her a minute, then looks at me. She shakes her head. "Females."

"You're preaching to the choir," I say. Then add, "Don't be too hard on her. This procedure didn't just save my life. It might've saved Gwen's, too."

Callie's anger fades the slightest bit. "What do you mean?"

"According to Dr. P., an object like this, placed where it was, receiving electronic signals—could have had a lethal effect on Gwen's heart. Not to mention it significantly increased her chances of developing breast cancer."

Callie says, "I wish Phyllis Willis was still alive."

"What would you do to her?"

"Very bad things."

She looks at Gwen and sighs. "Men are so much easier."

"Especially us gorgeous ones," I say.

Callie gives me a look I've seen before. Staring into her eyes, I can literally see the light draining out of them. All emotion has left her face. She's completely detached. It's amazing how the most beautiful creature in the world can look so devoid of human warmth. This is Callie's death face. It's how she looks when people are about to die.

When she speaks, her tone is flat. "The day our friendship ends?" she says.

"I know."

"Say it."

"Our friendship ends the day I call you sugar snatch."

She holds my gaze a full minute. It's such an uncomfortable minute, I finally say, "I'll never even think those words again."

"Yes you will. You'll think them every time you see me for the rest of our lives." She looks at Gwen. "Thanks to *you*."

Gwen puts her lower lip out, like a child who's been caught telling a family secret.

Callie looks back at me. "But you won't say those words out loud."

"I won't."

"Ever."

"Ever."

13.

One Week Earlier...
Maybe Taylor.

THE MAN WHO likes to be called Daddy said Professor Jonah Toth could be found teaching civics at Viceroy College in Charleston, South Carolina. Maybe didn't ask why Daddy wanted him dead. *You're not supposed to ask*, he'd told her months ago, shortly after they began their unusual telephone friendship. That was fine with Maybe. It wouldn't help to be sidetracked by questions or doubt. She would trust Daddy, kill the man, and move forward, toward bigger and more important assignments. Lucrative ones.

This will be Maybe's first murder for hire. She's going to receive ten thousand dollars for what will probably amount to a few hours work. She's already received the down payment, along with the murder weapon, in the handbag wedged under the spare tire in the trunk of her rental car. Maybe doesn't know how Daddy managed it, nor does she care. What she's thinking is, *this is almost too easy!*

The handbag contains five thousand dollars in cash, and a handgun equipped with a silencer. She's been told she won't need to remove the gun from the purse, she can just reach in and start shooting. If she's within ten feet of the target, the bullets will pass through the handbag and into Toth's body with relative accuracy. Since the gun is small caliber, she should be prepared to take multiple shots.

It's Wednesday morning.

Maybe locates Toth's ten a.m. class and monitors it from the back row. Toth is in his forties and dresses as pretentiously as possible, with his tweed jacket, crew neck sweater and designer jeans. He wears his dark brown hair seventies style, and has a short, well-groomed beard. All that's missing to complete the picture of what a hip professor is supposed to look like is a pipe.

Professor Toth's class is as boring as most of the classes Maybe attended her freshman and sophomore years. It's classes like this that made it easy to leave college after her second year. When his lecture finally ends, Maybe's one of the last students to file out. She lingers fifty feet down the hall, holding her large handbag to her chest. For this occasion she's wearing a cinnamon-colored wig and non-prescription Sarah Palin glasses.

Maybe's plan is to follow Professor Toth at a distance and wait until a killing opportunity presents itself. She's prepared to tail him all day and half the night, if necessary, but she catches an amazing break when Toth exits the classroom and walks into the men's room directly across the hall!

Don't professors pee in the teacher's lounges?

Apparently not always.

Maybe seizes the opportunity, and quietly slips into the bathroom after giving him a twenty second head start. The bathroom is laid out with two sinks on the right wall as you enter, then a divider, and four urinals beyond the divider. On the left, across from the urinals, are two stalls. Maybe can't believe her good fortune. They're alone in the men's room, she's at the sink, he's peeing at one of the urinals behind the divider, and neither can see the other. But she can hear him peeing. She removes the gun from her handbag, even though she was told not to. But Maybe's thinking if they're interrupted, she can shoot her way out of the bathroom, if necessary. She turns the water on in the sink so Toth will think someone's washing his hands, and then moves behind him, as if planning to use one of the stall toilets.

Toth never turns his head, content to stare straight ahead at the cement block wall eight inches in front of his face. Probably been taught all his life not to look around in case some other guy thinks you're checking him out.

It occurs to Maybe that this is one of the great differences between men and women. A woman will always turn her head to see who's entered the bathroom.

Maybe watches Toth moving his right hand up and down and realizes he's shaking his penis. *How odd*, she thinks. She's never had a penis, and hasn't seen but a few in her life, but she can't imagine it requires that much effort to get the last few drops of pee out. When Toth tucks his butt to stuff his mighty sword back in his pants, she walks right up behind him and fires two shots in the back of his head from less than a foot away.

Big mistake.

Maybe's never shot anyone before, and hasn't allowed for blood spatter. It's everywhere, including her face. There's so much blood she can hardly see out of her glasses.

But she can see enough.

She steps out of the way while Toth falls to the floor. He lands sideways, and rolls onto his back, and...

He's still alive!

The back of his head is gone, and the man is still alive! His mouth is moving like a baby bird that's waiting for its mama to drop a worm into it. *What a wondrous machine the human body is*, Maybe thinks, as she squeezes another shot into the space between his eyes. She goes to the sink, checks herself in the mirror, removes the bloody windbreaker she'd worn to give the impression of being twenty pounds heavier.

She stuffs the jacket in her purse, along with the glasses, and quickly scrubs her hands and face with soap, water, and paper towels. Then she stuffs the towels in her purse and heads out the bathroom door at a brisk pace.

14.

"HI DADDY," MAYBE says to the voice mailbox. "I kissed a professor!"

Five minutes later her cell phone rings.

"*Already?*" he says.

"Yup."

"Tell me about it."

She does.

Then he says, "Is there anything else you want to tell me?"

"There were no witnesses."

"You were lucky."

"I was good."

"You *were* good," he says. "Now tell me about Dr. Scott."

Maybe smiles. "What about him?"

"He's dead."

"No!" she says. "Tell me it's not true!"

"Talk to me, Maybe."

"I like it when you use my name."

"It's not your name. It's the name you chose."

"Still, you usually call me Baby."

"Tell me about Dr. Scott."

"What is there to tell?"

"I thought the therapy was working."

"You thought wrong."

"How'd you do it?"

"What do your sources say?"

"I don't have sources. I'm a hacker. I find things out the hard way. The reports are inconclusive."

"Inconclusive is good."

"Apparently, you've come up with a way to kill people that's undetectable, at least till toxicology comes back."

"Are you impressed?"

"Mildly. But they found the injection site, so it won't take long. What might they find?"

"They might find a high concentration of nutmeg in his system."

"Nice. Did you distill it yourself?"

"You're starting to sound impressed."

"I *am* impressed. It's a poison that can be found in anyone's spice cabinet. They'll never be able to trace it back to you."

"What else did the report say?"

"Dr. Scott was found dead in his office lying face down on the floor."

"Anything else?"

"His pants were pulled down to his knees and a giant dildo had been pounded into his rectum."

"You should've heard him scream."

"Why would they use the term 'pounded?'"

"There was a toolkit in his supply closet. With a large rubber mallet."

"You should've told me you killed him."

"Why?"

"To warn me."

"You're either good enough to take precautions, or you're not," Maybe says, indignantly.

"I took the necessary precautions."

"Such as?"

"I used a fake name and a different bank for every check. Sent them from different places, disguised my voice. Used throwaway cell phones for each call. I don't make mistakes."

"So what's the problem?"

"The problem is trust. You could've burned me."

"I trusted you to be prepared. Was I wrong?"

Daddy says nothing.

Maybe says, "Look. I killed him because he deserved to die. I didn't tell you because I wanted to see how good you were. Why would I want to deal with someone who can't protect himself?"

"And now you know I can."

"So far."

"You're as much as telling me I can't trust you."

"What do you expect from me? I'm a homicidal maniac!"

"You're a precious young lady."

"Seriously? *You're* the one who's turning me into a cold-blooded killer. How do you hope to trust me?"

"By having a special relationship with you."

"You know what I think, Daddy?"

"What's that?"

"I think you want to fuck me."

He pauses a long time. Then says, "I do. Is that so wrong?"

"It is if you make me call you Daddy."

"There's a reason for that."

"I know. It's called manipulation."

"Yes."

"When are you going to show yourself."

"In time."

"What are you, disfigured or something? Twice my age? You don't *sound* twice my age."

"I'm fifteen years and six days older than you."

Maybe pauses. That's the most personal information he's ever given her. She says, "If you're thirty-five, I'm going to call you Ralph."

"Ralph?"

"You sound like a Ralph."

He sighs. "You think you're ready?"

"For what?"

"The big time?"

"Lay it on me, Ralph."

15.

Present Day...
Donovan Creed.

"HELLO, FATHER."

"Kimberly! Hi!"

First time in what seems like forever my daughter Kimberly has actually taken my phone call. I wonder why now, and not the last dozen times over the past three months.

I start with what I hope is a safe topic. "How's college life?"

"My biology teacher's a dick."

"That should make for an interesting year-book picture."

"Tip-tip, pshhh!" she says, making a sound like a drummer hitting two rim shots and a cymbal.

"You must be dating again," I say. "I haven't heard from you in awhile."

"That's a nice way of saying I haven't answered or returned your calls."

"I try not to take it personally."

"Good. Yes, I'm dating. But you wouldn't approve."

"Why not?"

"Fathers never approve of the men in their daughters' lives."

"I can try."

"Right. Where are you this time?"

"Las Vegas."

"Winning much?"

"It's not that type of trip. What's his name?"

"My boyfriend? You can't *possibly* think I'd tell you that!"

"Why not?"

"Every time I tell you a boyfriend's name, he turns up dead."

"That happened *one* time! And you know very well the police said a woman did the shooting. A woman your boyfriend picked up at a bar and tried to rape!"

"He's an atheist."

"What? Who?"

"The guy I'm dating."

"An atheist?"

"Are you going to be judgmental about it?" she says. "Because if you are, I can hang up."

"Relax." I sigh. "Is that what defines him?"

"What do you mean?"

"I mean, is that how he introduces himself? 'Hi, Kimberly, I'm Chuck, the atheist!'"

She laughs. "Chuck?"

"Well, you won't tell me his name."

"You can call him Chuck. I like that. He's quite successful, by the way."

"Then, Chuck it is. Where'd you meet him?"

"At church."

"Excuse me?"

She laughs. "It's his job. He sells only to religious people."

I remove the phone from my ear and look at it. Sometimes a deliberate action like this proves I'm not dreaming. I put the phone back to my ear and say, "Please tell me why religious people buy products from an atheist."

"He's a pre-Rapture pet salesman."

I say nothing.

"Father? Hello-o? Are you still there?"

"Sorry. I thought you said he was a pre-Rapture pet salesman."

"You don't approve. I *knew* it!"

"I don't even know what it means."

She sighs. "You've heard of the Rapture, yes?"

"I have."

"Pets can't go."

"Where?"

"To heaven."

"They can't?"

"According to these people, they cannot."

"So?"

"So Chuck tells the church people he's not qualified to be part of the Rapture because he's an atheist, but he'll take care of their pets when they get called to heaven. For a fee."

"And they trust him?"

"He's a good salesman. Plus, he's the only game in town."

"And you're *dating* this guy?"

"We're not getting *married*, or anything. It's just sex right now."

"Thanks for sharing that."

"I figured you'd get around to asking, eventually."

"Have I ever asked about your sex life?"

"Not in so many words."

We're both quiet a moment. Then I say, "But school is good?"

Kimberly laughs.

"What's so funny?"

"Your ability to communicate with me leaves a lot to be desired!"

"Why is that, do you suppose?"

"I think you're afraid you'll say the wrong thing and I'll hang up. As usual."

"It doesn't mean I don't love you," I say, "because I do, and always have."

"I believe you. Even if you hate my boyfriend."

"*Hate* him? I don't even *know* him!"

"That's the point. But if we're being honest, what's your first impression?"

I pause. Then say, "He sounds like a flake."

"They're all flakes to you," she says. "And that's why I don't take your calls sometimes."

She hangs up, and I stare at my phone again before clicking it off.

Then I call Lou Kelly.

16.

"HOW'D THE BOARD meeting go?" Lou says.

"You did a good job with the information. They're probably scrambling to figure out a way to block Gwen."

"You don't really expect them to put her on the board, though, right?"

"No. But I expect they'll approach me to buy her out at a discount."

"Will she go for that?"

"She needs to. The company's about to go under. Anything she gets now is a plus. I'll work it all out."

"I'm sure you will. What's up?"

"My daughter, Kimberly."

"That sounds ominous."

"Do you know how to find the guy we used to have following her?"

"That was more than a year ago."

"Right. But he did a good job for us."

"Want me to track him down? Pay him whatever he wants?"

"Yeah. What's his name?"

"Jimmy T."

"Right. Good, solid guy. Let's get him back on the job. And also, I've got a funny feeling about her school."

"What about it?"

"Can you send me a copy of her grades for the past few semesters?"

"You think she quit?"

"I hope not, but it wouldn't shock me. She's quite a bullshitter, my daughter."

"Wonder where she inherited that skill?"

"Right. Problem is, I never know if she's making fun of me or being sincere. But she's dating another flake, and I'd feel better knowing Jimmy's keeping an eye on her. From a distance, of course."

"Last time we did that—"

"Yeah, I know. But still."

"In my experience with daughters—"

"I know. But I just spoke to her. Something's not right."

"You think she's in danger? We could kill the kid like last time."

"I just want our guy to keep an eye on her, maybe track this guy down, check him out."

We go quiet a few seconds. Then Lou says, "She still at Mabry Community College? Jacksonville?"

"That's what she claims."

"You don't believe her?"

"I'm not sure what to believe. She's got this attitude lately. I don't respond to it very well."

"She's found your buttons. Starting to push them."

"Exactly."

"Okay, I'm on it."

"Thanks, Lou."

I hang up, think about something, call him back.

"Forget something?" Lou says.

"Quick question."

"Shoot."

63

"You know anything about the Rapture?"

"The rap group? The book? The movie? The Bible?"

"The Bible."

"Like what?"

"You know if pets can go?"

"Where?"

"Heaven."

He pauses. "I'll check it out."

"Wait. You're not going to ask why I want to know?"

Lou laughs. "Nothing you could say would help me understand."

"Good point."

"Plus, I want to figure it out for myself."

"Are you that bored?"

"Last time you called me was a week ago. I could've been in the Bahamas all this time."

"You're breaking my heart."

"What heart?"

"Good point. Again."

17.

"WE'RE FRIENDS, RIGHT?"

Carmine "The Chin" Porrello, west coast mob boss, is on the phone. Wants to know if we're friends.

"That's a tough one," I say.

He chuckles. "Well, I were you, I'd say yes."

"Then, yes."

"'Cause this is a friendship call."

"Good to know," I say.

"I don't approve of you bustin' in my house."

"I know."

"On the other hand, you could've killed me, and you didn't."

"And I paid you fifty grand."

"True," he says. "Plus, I hear our friend survived the shooting."

He's talking about Gwen.

"She did," I say.

"You datin' her?"

"It's up in the air."

"Women, right?"

"Tell me why you're calling."

"You young people," he says.

"What about us?"

"You're too impatient. You don't understand the art of chit-chat."

"There's an art to chit-chat?"

"See? You don't know."

I feel like reaching through the phone and pulling the purpose of his call from his throat. He's right. I don't like idle chit-chat. I'd rather have a root canal. I'm sitting on a cot in the windowless room I built in the center of PhySpa, talking on the phone to a guy who's so old, last time I saw him his nuts were hanging out of his underwear and he didn't even know it. Until the phone buzzed, I'd been holding the ceramic device we recovered from Gwen's boob a few hours ago. Working it around in my hand the same way I used to work the silver dollar my grandfather gave me all those years ago. I wonder why I keep playing with this device instead of smashing it with a sledge hammer like any intelligent person would do. For some reason I'm content to hold this weapon of death in my hand. This device that can kill me instantly, should it fall into the wrong hands.

I wonder what that says about me.

Finally, after what seems like months, Carmine gets to the point.

"Someone wants to take out a hit on you."

"Thank goodness!"

"This news makes you happy?"

"Absolutely."

"Why?"

"It'll add excitement to my life."

"I didn't accept the hit."

"Why not?"

"Because we're friends."

"Oh."

We're quiet a minute. Then Carmine says, "Don't you wanna know?"

"What?"

"The person who wants you dead."

"No."

"Why not?"

"That'd make it too easy."

"I think you'll be surprised."

"I'm just messing with you," I say. "I already know who it is."

"Really?"

"Tony Spumoni. You know him?"

"Sure. He comes to the club."

"I embarrassed him today."

"How?"

"Ripped one of his ears off."

"No shit?" Carmine chuckles. "You're somethin' else, you are. That must've hurt."

"You'd think so. But you're right, I *am* surprised."

"Why's that?"

"There's a lot of uncertainty in his company. I'd expect him to wait till the dust clears."

We go silent again. Then Carmine says something that surprises me even more.

"It wasn't Tony."

"What?"

"It was your other business partner."

My *other* business partner? I frown. "Who, Wadsworth?"

"Nope."

I think a minute.

Of course!

Who stands to lose the most in the new business arrangement? The vice president of research and development.

"George Best," I say.

"I don't know Mr. Best," Carmine says.

"Okay, I give up. Who is it that wants me dead?"

"Our friend, Gwen Peters."

18.

WHAT? GWEN WANTS to put out a hit on me? *Why?*

That's what I want to say to Carmine. Instead I say, "You spoke to Gwen *personally*?"

"I knew you'd be surprised."

"You didn't answer my question."

"Yes, I spoke to her personally."

"No possibility you might be mistaken?"

"I've known her forever."

"Sometimes phones can be tricky," I say. "And face it, you're hard of hearing."

"Creed."

"Yeah?"

"I spoke to her in person."

"What?"

"She came to see me."

"When?"

"Ten minutes ago. She just left."

"Did you ask why?"

"Of course! Like I say, she and me, we go way back, you know?"

"What reason did she give?"

"She wouldn't. Said if she had to give me a reason, she'd take her business elsewhere."

I shake my head, move the device around in my hand some

more. I'm careful not to press the single button. There wasn't supposed to be a button, but there it is, right in the center. I was told the device attaches to a hand-held unit and can be reprogrammed with a new four-digit code. It can work that way, but as the others filed out of the board meeting today, George and William told me the board wants the device back. When I asked why, they explained it can be used on its own. In other words, if I press the button four times within ten seconds, it'll fry my brain. I told them they couldn't have it. I could keep it or turn it over to the police. They weren't happy about either possibility.

"You still there?" Carmine says.

I know why I'm feeling a little blue. My abandonment issues are kicking in. The device reminds me of my silver dollar, and the silver dollar reminds me of my original family, all of whom are dead, which reminds me how alone I am in the world. I know what you're thinking. I'm supposed to look on the bright side, right? Well, maybe you can help me find it. My ex-wife Janet hates me. My daughter Kimberly won't return my calls except to punish me. The woman I loved, Kathleen, is married to another guy. My girlfriend, Rachel, is a homicidal maniac. When we were together I had to drug her every night to keep her from killing me in my sleep! My close friend and facilitator, Lou Kelly, tried to kill me recently, which has severely impacted our working relationship. My boss at Homeland Security, Darwin, ordered a chip to be planted in my brain so he can kill me whenever it suits him. Callie, my best friend in the world, doesn't trust me. She used those exact words to describe our relationship recently, and gave me her death stare an hour ago.

And now Gwen wants to pay someone to kill me.

"What did you tell her?" I ask Carmine.

"I said I'd think about it."

"Doesn't sound like something a friend would say."

"If I gave her a quick no, she'd call someone else. This way you can nip it in the bud."

He's right.

"Thanks, Carmine."

"You're surprised, aren't you!"

I am.

"I owe you," I say.

"That's what I like to hear!"

The PhySpa phone rings, so I tell my friend, the mob boss, I've got to run.

"Come see me tonight," he says. "At the club."

"Which one?"

"*Top Six.*"

"When?"

"Ten."

I click off the cell phone and pick up the PhySpa phone.

"Who's this?" I say.

"Tony Spumoni."

"I was just talking about you," I say. "Your ears must've been burning."

"You think that's funny?"

I think it's hilarious. But what I say is, "What do you want?"

"I want to settle this thing between us."

"How?"

"I did some checking. I know who you are, what you do."

"So?"

"Can we meet tonight?"

"Why?"

"I got a proposition for you."

"You can't tell me over the phone?"

"I already said too much."

My cell phone vibrates. Lou Kelly. To Tony I say, "You know the club, *Top Six*?"

"Carmine Porrello's club?"

"Yeah."

"What time?"

"Ten-thirty."

I hang up the house phone, answer the cell. "That was quick."

"I'm going to take a stab at this," Lou says, laughing. "Kimberly's boyfriend's a pre-Rapture pet salesman, right?"

"You're good. You found him?"

"I don't know where to start. There are hundreds of these guys scattered across the country. I found six in Duval County. Their standard sales pitch is pets have no souls, so they'll be left behind when the Rapture takes place. If you love your pets, you won't let them starve."

"So Kimberly's boyfriend has to convince them he's sinful enough to be left behind but loving enough to care for their pets."

"Odd way to make a buck," Lou says.

"Anything else?"

"Kimberly's grades."

"Do I want to know?"

"You do."

"Lay it on me."

"Perfect attendance, A's in every subject but one."

"Biology?"

"Right. B plus."

"He's a dick."

"Who, the teacher?"

"Yeah."

"She said that?"

"She did."

"Kids talk like that to their parents these days?"

"I don't know how kids talk. Like we said, she's pushing my buttons."

"You say anything to her about it?"

"No. She's got all the power."

"How so?"

"She can hang up anytime she wants."

"You can stop sending her money."

"And what type of message would that send? Respect me or else?"

Lou pauses a minute. Then says, "Well, at least she's still enrolled, making good grades. That's a good thing. And she's always been a great kid."

"And still is," I say. "So yeah, I'm lucky. It could be a helluva lot worse. How about our guy, Jimmy T.?"

"You still want her followed?"

"For a little while. Until I'm completely comfortable about things."

"I'll track Jimmy down and put him to work."

"Thanks, Lou."

19.

I FOCUS A pinpoint of light on the face of my watch as it turns 9:00 p.m., thinking, *two hours ago Gwen Peters asked Carmine "The Chin" Porrello to have me whacked.*

I'm in the Las Vegas Zoo, standing by the monkey cage. The monkeys are so surprised to see a visitor after closing time, they actually stop picking their asses to stare at me.

"You talkin' to me?" I say, channeling my inner Robert DeNiro.

The zoo's been closed three hours. It was harder to break in than you'd think. Probably because they house endangered cats, apes, and exotic reptiles, so their security needs to be top notch.

It's dark, but not pitch black. I might need the pen light to see my watch, but I can see the monkeys without it, and they can see me. I snap the light off and put it back in my pocket, remove the ceramic device and move it around in my hand.

The monkey cage isn't actually a cage. It's more like a deep, circular pit with a rock mountain in the center, and some artificial climbing trees. The monkeys have lots of space to move around in, and the trees and mountain offer them opportunities to exercise. The chain link fence around the perimeter comes up to the middle of my chest, high enough to keep kids from falling into the pit.

I fling the ceramic device at the monkeys.

Several rush to the place where it strikes the mountain, and scramble around, fighting for it, until one emerges with the prize.

I watch with amusement as he tries to keep it away from the others. He jumps onto one of the trees and makes his way to the top. He sniffs it, puts it in his mouth. For a moment I think how funny it'll be if he swallows it. But he removes it from his mouth and works it around in his hand the way I've been doing.

Pressing the button four times in ten seconds will fry my brain.

The monkey gives up and tosses the device to the ground.

Dozens of monkeys begin fighting over it, and I assume it won't take long for this many monkeys to press a single button four times in ten seconds.

Why am I doing this?

I don't know. It's fun? I'm in Vegas? I need the rush? My fate is in the hands of a bunch of monkeys, which seems appropriate, somehow.

I start to laugh. And keep laughing. Kimberly's not the only one who can push my buttons!

"Have at it!" I shout, and walk away. I get about five feet when something hits me in the back of the head.

I bend down and pick up the device.

The monkeys have spoken.

I wipe the device on my pant leg, put it back in my pocket. Then head to Carmine Porrello's club, the *Top Six*.

20.

"HOW OLD IS that one?" I ask Carmine, pointing at the skinny blond on the far left.

"The nurse?"

I feel like saying, "nurse costume," but what's the point?

"You like her?" Carmine says.

"She doesn't look legal."

"I run a legit club. She don't look eighteen, but she's got a driver's license. You want me to call her over?"

"No."

I look at the skinny girl a second time. Her hair is close-cropped, with a streak of red on the front of each side, framing her delicate, pale face. She looks like she's completely drugged out. But there's something else in her face that would break my heart if I were her father. It's something you don't normally see at her age.

She's given up.

This is the type of kid who probably won't live to see her twenties. I'm looking at a dead girl, I think.

"You keep lookin' at her," Carmine says. "Here, I'll call her over."

He waves his hand until she notices him. She looks over her shoulder a minute, then back at Carmine, then reluctantly climbs off the stage and comes over.

"Hi Shirl," he says.

"Is something wrong?" she says. "I'm supposed to go on next."

"Don't worry about it."

Shirl looks nervously to the left of the stage. "But Roy—"

"I'll take care of Roy."

She looks dubious.

Carmine says, "You trust me, yes?"

"Yes, of course, Mr. Porrello."

He nods. "Good. I want you to meet a friend of mine. A good friend."

She looks at me. I notice Carmine didn't say my name, which is his way of showing respect. He's old school. He'll let me decide if I want to use a fake name.

"Hi Shirl, I'm Donovan Creed."

I put my hand out. Shirl looks at me with utter confusion, bites the corner of her lip and looks at Carmine, who says, "He's offering you his hand. Shake it."

Shirl looks completely bewildered, but takes my hand. It took her exactly ten seconds to make me feel like I'm mentally challenged. She looks back up at the stage, clearly agitated, shifting her weight from one leg to the next, while looking at the big, angry slab of beef who's giving her a hard look.

"That's Roy?" I say.

"Uh huh. I better go."

She starts to move, but Carmine puts his hand on her arm. Shirl stops, but looks as though she might pee her pants, she's so frightened.

"Don't be rude," Carmine says.

"We're about to play PNQ," she says, by way of explanation. "I'm up first."

Carmine nods. "Okay. After that, you come back down."

"I'll ask Roy."

"You'll *what*?" Carmine says.

Shirl realizes she's made a big mistake. By fearing Roy more than Carmine, she's disrespected the old Don.

In front of me, a good friend.

She's in full-blown panic mode. It's pitiful to see.

I know what's going on here. Carmine's older than dirt. Roy's the young tough. They're about to butt heads. Carmine, needing to prove he's still got it. Roy, not wanting to be disrespected. I'm in a position to prevent it. Normally I wouldn't give a shit either way, but Carmine did me a favor telling me about Gwen. And this little girl shouldn't have to live in fear like this.

"What's PNQ?" I say.

Carmine's about to blow up, but my question simmers him down a bit. He actually starts to chuckle.

"PNQ stands for penny, nickel, quarter. It's a game our friend Gwen made up when she used to work for me. Since you never played, I don't wanna give nothin' away. You'll like it."

"I'll walk Shirl back up on stage," I say.

Carmine starts to say something, then looks over at Roy, who's scowling at both of us. Then says, "That's good." He smiles, and adds, "That's *real* good. And Creed?"

"Yes, Mr. Porrello?" I say, showing him respect in front of Shirl because I, too, am old school.

"Have fun with it," he says.

"You know it."

21.

"WHATEVER YOU'RE ABOUT to do on stage," I say to Shirl, "You don't have to."

"It's okay."

"I'm serious."

"Me too. Of all the things I have to do, this is the easiest. It's no big deal, and it's fun for the customers."

"What about afterward?"

"After PNQ?"

"Yes."

"That part's not so much fun. But it's work, you know?"

"I do."

By now, Shirl and I have climbed the side steps to the stage, and Jimmy comes over to meet us. The Emcee has been watching this mini drama unfold, and he's stalling, telling jokes, to buy a little time.

Roy's furious. His reptilian eyes have narrowed to slits, and the veins in his temples are pulsing. But he doesn't say anything yet. He doesn't know me, but figures I'm connected, since Carmine called Shirl over to meet me. But he's connected too, and he's a certified tough guy, something I can tell by the scar tissue around his eyes, and the fact his nose has been broken at least twice. Up in his hairline I see a thin line where he's had surgery. If I'm guessing, that's from a beer bottle. Bouncing's a tough life. Roy's got to be happy he's moved up a step, running strippers. Helluva lot easier beating up young girls than tough drunks.

The three of us are standing on the stage, just beyond the steps. Shirl's nervous. I'm sizing up this young, stocky warrior, and Roy's probably doing the same to me. He's waiting for me to speak, but I'm in no hurry. They're on a time clock here, not me.

Roy says, "Get your ass center stage, you piece of shit."

Shirl moves quickly. As she passes him, he puts his leg out and trips her. She stumbles, but shows remarkable athleticism correcting her fall at the last second. She manages to keep from hitting the stage. He snarls, "You and me are gonna have a little talk tonight."

She looks at me.

I nod back.

"You got something to say to me, asshole?" he asks me.

"Nope."

"Then get your ass back with grandpa before I kick the shit outta you."

"Yes, sir!"

"Well?"

"Well what?"

"You're still here."

"I am?"

He pauses. Then says, "You don't want to piss me off."

"Of course not."

"Then get the fuck outta my club."

"Wait. I thought you wanted me to get my ass back with grandpa."

He shows me that look people give when they wonder if I'm some kind of wise ass.

"What're you, some kind of wise ass?" he says.

"Yeah, but it's not all it's cracked up to be."

He makes a sudden move, hoping to catch me off-balance, to push me backwards. There are only four steps, but we're high enough that a push could cause serious injury.

No matter. I've been expecting the shove since Roy joined us. Most bar fighters want to shove you before launching their power shot. It gets you off balance, gets your hands away from your face, so they can inflict the most possible damage before you can retaliate. If they get you on the ground it can be a rough night if you're unskilled.

Unfortunately for Roy, I'm plenty skilled. Before his right hand makes contact with my chest, I reach up and grab it with my left hand and start squeezing. Roy's been around tough guys all his life, but he's never had his hand stuck in a vice grip like mine, and it shows in his expression as I crush the bones in his hand. He screams in pain and tries to get his hand away, which only makes it worse for him, because it gives me the opportunity to clamp down harder.

In the background, I hear the emcee go quiet. The whole club is watching us, but Carmine's holding a hand up, to keep them from interfering. I turn my attention back to Roy. His eyes are bugging out. As he begins to panic, he makes another blunder by moving his body into mine, attempting to muscle me down the steps. But before Roy's chest makes contact with my body, I grab his belt with my right hand and spin us around to where our positions are reversed. I continue squeezing his hand, but now I'm also grinding the broken bones together. Tears are pouring from his eyes, and he's holding his left hand up in supplication, trying to get to his knees. I lower his hand enough to accommodate him.

Now, with Roy on his knees, I lean over and whisper in his ear, "You don't hit Shirl, you don't touch her, ever again.

You got that?"

I squeeze his hand harder, for emphasis. Then back it down slightly so he won't pass out.

"I *got* it!" he gasps.

"If you so much as raise your voice to her, I'll hear about it, and you'll regret it. Tell me you understand."

He nods his head, vigorously. "I understand," he says.

Roy really *is* a tough guy. I've crushed the bones in his hand so badly it's going to require extensive surgery to correct. In a few years he'll probably end up with the worst case of arthritis imaginable. Roy's at a point where I could make him do anything. I consider making him sing 'Mammy', by Al Jolson. I mean, he's already on his knees, right? But that would be cruel. And anyway, I have a better idea.

"One last thing," I say.

Roy's trying not to cry in front of the whole bar. His tough guy persona is really taking a beating tonight, and he'll probably have to maim some drunks to re-establish his rep. I just hope he doesn't treat the other girls worse because he's angry at Shirl. I'm not going to threaten him about it, though. These girls, they come and go. They've been around the block. I'm not going to warn Roy not to pick on them. I don't know the other girls. They could make something up about him, and I wouldn't know the difference, and that wouldn't be fair. But there *is* something I need to warn him about that will be easy to monitor.

"You're disrespecting Carmine," I say. "And I won't have it. He made his bones before your parents were born. In other words, he's earned his place. I'm going to let go of you, and when I do, you're going to walk over to Carmine and kiss his ring. And Roy?"

He looks up at me.

"If you don't, I'm going to kill you before the sun comes up."

He looks down. Then back up.

"Do you believe me?"

He nods through his tears.

I release his hand and watch him walk over to Carmine with his head bowed. When he gets there, he apologizes, and kneels to kiss Carmine's ring. As he does so, Carmine slaps the side of his face, hard. There's not much force on the blow, since Carmine's old and out of shape, but it makes enough of a sound to fill the room.

Then Carmine stands and embraces Roy, and calls someone over to drive him to the hospital. When that's worked out, I rejoin Carmine at his table in front of the stage, and the emcee announces how the game is played.

22.

"LADIES AND GENTLEMEN, you're in for a treat," the emcee says, "because it's time to play PNQ!"

The rules are simple. Anyone who wants to play gets a card to fill out. The card costs ten dollars. Carmine insists I play, and buys me a card. At the top left is the number one, and beside it are pictures of a penny, a nickel, a quarter, a half-dollar, and a silver dollar. The pictures are repeated for numbers two through eight. There will be eight strippers on stage. The idea is to pick the smallest coin that can completely cover the aureole on the left breast of each girl.

We're given a marking pen to make our choices. Looks like thirty of us are playing. Winner gets half the pot and a lap dance from the stripper of his choice. The girl he chooses gets one-fourth of the pot, the house gets the rest.

First girl up is Shirl, wearing her nurse costume. She walks to the front of the stage and peels down to her bra and panties, which surprises me, because she's wearing an actual bra and panties instead of stripper gear. Gear's probably not the right word, but I don't know the lingo. I don't frequent stripper bars. They're too depressing. Take Shirl, for instance.

While she's up there, smiling, the men hoot and holler. She puts her arms in the air and moves for them, and ends her little dance by turning her backside toward the audience and shaking it. The men like what they see. They like it a lot.

This is why I don't do strip joints. I'm quite annoyed watching Shirl perform for these rowdy drunken customers like some sort of stage monkey. If I weren't Carmine's guest, I'd walk out right now. Of course, if I weren't Carmine's guest, I wouldn't have entered the *Top Six* in the first place. I watch Shirl play up to the men. She's facing us now, caressing herself, licking her lips while giving that universal bedroom look these women have all perfected. I can't imagine why Shirl would act like that.

Then it hits me.

She's trying to win the lap dance money.

I think about the emotions I've just experienced, and realize what a colossal hypocrite I am! Getting all worked up wondering how a girl like Shirl could do this. Wasn't it just this morning I had sex with Gwen, who danced on this very stage eight months ago? Look at me, Mr. High-and-Mighty, indignant about this poor waif. If Shirl was two years older and a little prettier, I'd almost certainly pay her for sex tonight.

I think about Kimberly, and how she wanted to shock me by telling me she's having sex with the pet salesman. I wonder how shocked she'd be to learn I've been dating a 20-year-old hooker named Miranda.

When she's done milking the crowd, Shirl moves down the stage, not far from where we had the altercation with Roy a few minutes ago. With nothing to go on but a hunch, I put an X on the picture of the penny, meaning, I think when she takes her top off later, the aureole circling her nipple will prove to be smaller than a penny.

Next girl up is Tina. She's heavy, maybe five-four, one-eighty. She's wearing a cow girl outfit, but again, a real bra and panties. I put her down for the half-dollar. Third is Allison, who's about thirty. Allison's dressed in a business suit, complete with reading glasses. I figure her for a quarter.

The game continues through the progression of eight, then several guys go through the crowd, inspect the cards, sign them, and collect the pens. The emcee calls out "Girl number one!"

Shirl comes to the front of the stage and removes her bra. Guys are yelling now. Some are screaming "Penny!" Others, "Nickel!" They're all claiming to be right. The emcee makes a few demeaning jokes about the size of her chest that piss me off, then Shirl produces a coin, pushes it onto her nipple, ending all speculation.

Shirl's a nickel.

Guys are hollering at each other in a good-natured way.

Carmine smiles. "Helluva game, right? Really gets the crowd worked up. Great for business!"

"Gwen came up with this idea?" I say.

"She did."

I'm thinking Gwen's creativity might be a good thing for Ropic Industries. Then I remember she doesn't want me around to see it.

The heavy set girl, Tina, amazingly, is a penny.

"You're not very good at this, are you?" Carmine says.

I shrug.

Allison, the business woman, is indeed a quarter.

"One out of three!" I say, more enthusiastically than I would've expected.

By the time the last woman proves her size, I end up with a paltry two out of eight. I'm amazed to see three men on their feet, holding up their cards, claiming to have gotten them all. One of the winners is Tony Spumoni.

He's got an enormous cast covering one side of his head. Looks ridiculous.

"You did that to his ear?" Carmine says.

"How's it possible three guys got them all?" I ask, realizing I'm more interested in the contest than Tony's condition. What does *that* say about me?

"They're regulars," Carmine says. "We always bring in one or two housewives to make it interesting, but the rest are our girls."

"So the system rewards those who support the club day in and day out."

"Pretty clever, right?"

It *is* clever. Proving Gwen has a lot more going for her than a great face and killer body.

Before they bring the next stripper out to break the tie, Carmine says, "Come with me."

We get to our feet and start walking toward his office. As I pass Tony I say, "I'll meet you after you collect your lap dance."

He nods.

In Carmine's office, I move the chair he wants me to sit in so that I have a clear view of his office and bathroom doors.

"It's in your nature to disrespect me," he says.

"Too much respect can get a guy killed."

23.

"REASON I WANTED to talk to you," Carmine says, "this thing with little Gwennie has my stomach all tied up in knots."

"I know how you feel."

"You been fuckin' her," he says. He puts his hand up. "You don't have to answer. It's between the two of you. I also know she had something to do with killing Lucky. Figure your girl's the one who did it. What's her name? Callie something?"

I say nothing.

He waves his hand. "Whatever. None of my business. I'm an old man."

"You've still got teeth," I say, referring to his power.

He chuckles. "A few." Then he says, "That was nice of you, crushing Roy's hand like that." He chuckles again. "Bad for Roy, though."

"You gave him a good slap."

"I should'a killed him." He sighs. "In the old days…" his voice trails off.

"What about little Gwennie?" I say.

"That," he says. "I gotta wonder. How did things get so bad between you?"

I shrug. "Tell you the truth, I thought we were getting along really well."

He nods. "Women, right?"

"The smart move is to kill her."

He nods. "I know." He pauses, looks at me.

"What?"

"I'm an old man," he says.

"You said that."

"See? Old people repeat themselves." He laughs. "Anyway, what I was gonna say, this thing that's got her angry, whatever it is, maybe you can work it out between you. What I'm sayin', you got a little time here. Maybe you can figure it out. I don't know. Buy her flowers, a mink coat, you know?"

"Women don't wear mink these days."

"No?"

"No."

"Why not?"

"Does it matter?"

He slaps his hand against his forehead. "No wonder I can't get any pussy!"

We laugh. Then I say, "You really think if I bring her flowers she won't try to have me killed?"

"How the fuck do I know? What I *do* know is, you give a woman a gift, it forces her to speak to you."

"She spoke to me today. Many times."

"Was she mad?"

"Quite the opposite."

"She catch you cheating?"

"Nope."

He shrugs. "Women, right?"

"Women," I say.

We're quiet a while, two guys in the office of a strip club, wondering how we could possibly know so little about women.

"Don't tell her I said anything," Carmine says.

"I wouldn't do that."

He nods. We both know it's important for Gwen to believe she has his confidence.

I say, "She offer you money?"

"For the hit? Nah. We didn't get that far."

"Because?"

He looks at me. "I told you."

"Yeah. We're friends. I know. But why didn't you take the hit? You know she'll inherit money from the estate. Eventually."

"Don't dismiss the friendship part so easily."

I wait.

He says, "The other part is, I got no one good enough. I can't afford to lose any more shooters."

Finally. An honest answer.

Carmine says, "Did you know Tony was gonna be here tonight?"

"He's the one that called when I was on the phone with you. He wants to talk."

"Do me a favor?"

"Name it."

"You decide to tear off his other ear, do it outside, okay? Customers see that sort of thing, it's bad for business."

"Got it. No tearing off ears inside the club."

He stares at me a moment. Then says, "How do you do it?"

"What, tear a guy's ear off?"

"Yeah. What I'm askin', does it come off clean?"

"With practice."

He looks at me like a proud father looks at his son after watching him hit a game-winning home run. Then chuckles. "You kids these days. Jeez."

I smile. Truth is, it only requires seven pounds of pressure to rip a guy's ear off his head. Take a dozen sheets of typing paper, hold them together with one hand, tear them with the other. That's an equivalent effort. The trick is to hook your fingers as far behind the ear as possible, grabbing as much tissue as you can. Don't try to pull the ear off. There's too much connective tissue. You want to tear from the top of the ear downward. At first you might have problems shearing the entire ear off in one motion. Like I say, it takes practice.

24.

"LET'S TAKE IT outside," Tony says.

We're standing at the end of the bar. He's looking past me, watching a young pole dancer. His eyes widen slightly. I turn to follow his gaze. She's upside down on the pole, doing a split.

"Talented girl," he says.

I wonder if he's got some thugs in the parking lot, waiting to ambush me.

"We can talk here," I say.

"It's too public. What I want to say requires privacy."

"Follow me," I say.

We go down the hall. When we get to the bathroom, I open the door.

"After you," I say.

"What? We can't meet in the friggin' *bathroom*," he says.

"Why not? I can keep people out."

He looks at me like I'm insane. Doesn't bother me. I probably *am* insane. He enters the room, I follow close behind. When the door's closed he says, "Creed."

"Yeah?"

"Should I call you Donovan?"

I shake my head. Poor, pitiful Tony.

"You're right," I say. "Let's take it outside."

When we get outside, I motion him to join me in my rental

car. He looks around a minute, then climbs in. Before he can speak, I punch his temple and he goes out like a light. I start the car and drive to the edge of the parking lot and wait till traffic is moving at a good clip. Then I floor the gas pedal, squeal the tires, and force my way into the line of fast-moving cars. While I'm doing this I reach over and rip Tony's shirt open, pull the microphone off his chest, and throw it in the street. Then I cross lanes, reverse direction, and roar past the detectives as they're leaving the parking lot, heading the wrong way.

When Tony starts coming around, I punch him again. Next time he comes around, we're in the parking lot of Wildrose Memorial. I get out, walk around the front of the car, open the passenger door.

"Where are we?" Tony says, looking around.

"Quick lesson, sport. Next time you wear a wire, don't start the conversation by asking the mark his name."

"They *made* me say your name like that! We *practiced*!"

"Yeah? Well, I've been practicing, too!"

I pull him out of the car, grab his good ear between my thumb and fingers, and tear it cleanly from his head. It's a vile, messy business, this ear-tearing thing. Generates far more blood than you'd expect. As Tony starts to go into shock, I hand him his ear and point him toward the E.R.

I start heading to George Best's house, but get sidetracked by Callie's phone call.

"Mr. Cohen?" she says. "There are two detectives at my condo. Is there any way you can meet me?"

I look at my watch. "This time of night? They must think they have something."

Callie says nothing, so I say, "I can come right now, but I don't have my lawyer business card with me."

"That'll be fine," she says. Then adds, "They don't understand why you're representing both Gwen and me."

I smile. Callie makes it easy to read between the lines. "I'll be glad to explain it to them when I get there."

"Thanks, Mr. Cohen." She tells me her address and what floor she's located on, since the attorney, Mr. Cohen, wouldn't know.

"I'll be there in five minutes," I say.

25.

I'VE GOT A key to get in, but we don't want the detectives to know that, so I buzz Callie's penthouse and she clicks the lobby lock open. I take the elevator to the top floor and knock on her door. When she opens it, I see two plainclothes detectives looking very disgusted by my presence on the scene. They look so much alike, they could be brothers. One has a brown suit on, the other's wearing navy. Both are wearing ties. Callie leads us into the living room. I study Gwen's face for any sign that might indicate she asked Carmine to kill me. But her expression offers nothing. I catch myself thinking she'd make a great agent for me, if I could trust her a little more. Or at all.

"Don't worry boys," I say to the detectives. "You're going to love the way I work."

"Oh yeah?" brown suit says. "Why's that?"

"Because I'm going to let my clients answer all your questions."

"You're what?"

"That's right. They've got nothing to hide."

"If that's the case," navy suit says, "you don't need to be here at all."

"True. Except that my presence will keep you on your best behavior."

"I've never seen you, never heard of you," brown suit says.

95

"You got proof of representation?"

"My proof is my client called me and asked me to come. When I got here, she let me in."

"I'm—"

I wave him off. "Look, I don't care what your names are. You're brown suit, he's navy suit. I'm Carlos Cohen."

"Carlos?"

"Yeah, that's right."

Brown suit starts to say something, thinks better of it. Turns to Gwen and says, "You don't seem very upset about your husband's death."

"I'm not."

The detectives look at me, stunned. Not only have I allowed Gwen to incriminate herself, I motion them to continue.

They look at each other.

Blue suit shrugs and says, "Your husband was murdered in cold blood and you're not upset? Why?"

They look at me again. When I continue to say nothing, brown suit says, "Are you sure you're a lawyer?"

"I knew you'd love working with me. Just wait till you hear her confession!"

"Her what?"

To Gwen I say, "You may answer the detective's question."

"I didn't love my husband," Gwen says. "He lied to me, and cheated on me."

Brown suit is so befuddled, he has to regroup.

Blue suit says, "Mrs. Peters, do you own a handgun?"

"Nope."

He turns to Callie and says, "Do you?"

"Do I look like the kind of woman who needs a handgun?"

Both suits look at me.

"Please answer the question, Miss. Carpenter."

"No. I don't own a handgun."

"May we verify that fact by conducting a quick search?"

"Define 'quick,'" I say.

"A cursory search. Ten minutes, max."

"That's all you need?"

"That's all we need."

I look at Callie. She nods. "I'll allow it, subject to ground rules. You stay together, we go where you go. No questions during the search. You've got ten minutes, starting now."

Ten minutes later blue suit says, "We can wrap this up in five minutes."

"You're done," I say. "My clients have been completely cooperative, and we utilized your time frame."

"We can come back with a search warrant," brown suit threatens.

"I wish I could be there when you ask the judge."

"Why?"

"Because you asked for ten minutes to search the premises. I asked if that was all you needed and you said yes. My clients consented to the search. You did, in fact, search the premises, and found nothing."

"There's sufficient cause to conduct a more thorough search."

"This will be fun to hear. Please enlighten us."

Brown suit points at Gwen. "Her husband was murdered in her house." He points at Callie. "And her lover was murdered at the same time."

"Is that your sufficient cause?"

"Probable cause," blue suit corrects.

"And did you just now learn that both my clients were connected to the victims?"

"We knew it the night of the murder," brown suit says.

"Which means you knew it before you asked for ten minutes to conduct your search," I say. "So you've already used up your probable cause search."

They don't like what they're hearing, but they're veterans. While I may be confusing them, I'm not intimidating them.

Brown suit says, "You may be right. We can let the judge decide."

"Then let's," I say.

We go back into Callie's living room.

"Miss. Carpenter," brown suit says. "Was Eva LeSage your lover?"

"I'm not going to answer any questions I've covered with the police. Gwen and I have cooperated fully, and you know these answers. I'll give you a quick synopsis, and then you can either ask me something new, that no one has asked during the last four sessions, or you can leave."

"Let's hear the synopsis," blue suit says.

"Eva and I were lovers. Lucky Peters hired Eva for three-way sex on Tuesdays. Sometimes Gwen participated, sometimes she didn't. Gwen and Eva were friends, which is how Gwen and I met and became lovers. On the Tuesday night they were murdered, Gwen and I were here in my apartment. You've spoken to the neighbors. They told you we were here all evening."

"They told us *you* were here all evening."

"That's because Gwen was already in the house when they saw me come home that afternoon."

"Can you prove it?"

"My proof is she's alive."

"That doesn't mean anything. She could've killed them."

"Right," Gwen says. "That's exactly what happened. I killed the two bodyguards, killed Eva and Lucky, drove to

Callie's condo—wait—I must've flown here, because my car was and still is at my house. Anyway, I killed everyone with a gun I don't possess, flew here on my broomstick and entered Callie's condo in such a way that none of the neighbors heard or saw me."

"There's the confession I promised!" I say. "Now if you boys will go ahead and arrest Mrs. Peters, we can take it straight to the courtroom. And don't worry about a search warrant. We'll provide the broomstick now, so you can enter it into evidence."

Without batting an eye, blue suit says, "Mrs. Peters, do you know Carmine Porrello?"

Gwen looks me dead in the eyes, but I can't make anything out of her expression.

"Answer truthfully," I say.

"I know him," she says. "I used to dance in his clubs. So what?"

"The four victims were executed."

"What's that mean?"

"I was at the crime scene," brown suit says.

"So?"

"In the twenty-three years I've been on the force, this was the most professional hit I've ever seen."

"Oh. Oh *my*!" Gwen says. Her face starts to flush. She actually looks at Callie and smiles. She's proud of her girlfriend's work.

"Did you just smile?" blue suit says.

"I sure did!"

He looks at me.

"She's got a beautiful smile," I say. "Don't you agree?"

"Thanks, Mr. Cohen," Gwen says, brightly.

Blue suit looks at Gwen. "Why would that comment make

you smile?"

"Because it sounds like you might have a suspect. Carmine Porrello."

"When's the last time you saw Mr. Porrello?" blue suit says.

Gwen looks at me. For the first time, she appears nervous. We both know if they're asking they already know the answer. I wonder if they've had a tail on Gwen and Callie. Then realize they've probably got surveillance on Carmine's club.

"Answer truthfully," I say. "If you saw him this afternoon, tell them."

Both suits look at me, incredulously. But neither speaks.

Gwen says, "I saw Carmine this afternoon."

"Where?" blue suit says.

"His place. The *Top Six*."

"Why?"

Gwen locks eyes with me. "I wanted to ask him something."

"What?"

"I asked if he knew who killed my husband."

"And he said?"

"He said he didn't know."

Brown suit says, "What'd you expect him to say?"

Gwen looks at Brown suit with the most beguiling expression I've ever seen on a recently widowed woman and says, "Should I not have asked him?"

Both suits frown.

"Anything else boys?" I say.

After they leave, Callie says to Gwen, "Why did you meet Carmine Porrello today?"

26.

"CAN WE DISCUSS this later?" Gwen says. She pauses a moment, then adds, "In private?"

Callie and I exchange a look.

I say, "Callie and I are a team, Gwen. Whatever happens, you're not going to come between us."

"Is that true, Callie?" Gwen says.

Callie says nothing.

To me, Gwen says, "She doesn't need you, and I don't need you. You know what you are?"

"Tell me."

"A candy ass!"

I frown.

"Maybe you should put some oil around your ankles," she says.

"Why's that?"

"To keep the ants from getting to your candy ass!"

Gwen looks at Callie for approval.

Callie says, "Why did you meet Carmine Porrello today?"

"I wanted to ask him something."

"Go on."

Gwen looks at me again. "I wanted him to kill someone."

"Who?" Callie says.

Gwen nods at me and says, "Donovan."

Callie studies my face.

"You knew," she says.

"I did. What I don't know is why."

We look at Gwen. Callie says, "Why?"

Gwen sighs. "It's hard to explain."

"Try," I say.

She frowns at me. Then says, "I couldn't choose between you."

"What do you mean?" Callie says.

"I like you both. I mean, I like you better, Callie. You're beautiful, you're stable, you treat me great…"

"But?" Callie says.

"But today when I fucked Donovan, I felt terrible. Not at the time, of course, but…"

"Back up." Callie says. "You fucked Creed today?"

She looks at me.

"It's partly my fault," I say.

"Partly?"

"Mostly."

"So anyway," Gwen says, "afterward, I felt terrible. I really like Donovan, but I decided today I love you."

"Before or after you fucked him?"

"After."

Callie looks at me. "I would've expected better from you."

I shrug. "You had to be there."

To Gwen, Callie says, "You love me?"

"I do."

"How could I ever expect to trust you?"

"If Donovan dies, the problem goes away."

Callie looks at me and says, "Why is it all your girlfriends want to kill you?"

I shrug. "Some don't."

"So far as you know." She looks at Gwen. "We're not

killing Creed. Pack your things."

I say, "Callie? She knows everything."

Gwen says, "Wait. I would *never* tell!"

"The detectives aren't done with this," I say. "They might try to work on her."

"What about my T-shirt business?" Gwen says.

"It might raise some eyebrows at the next board meeting if she turns up dead," I say.

"They haven't approved the reorganization yet though, right?" Callie says.

"True."

Gwen starts backing up. "Can't we just forget what happened today?"

"Which part?" Callie says.

"All of it. I want a do-over. No more Donovan. Just you, Callie. For ever and always."

Callie says, "You sound sincere. But can I trust you?"

"Yes. I swear."

"If you ever cheat on me again, I'll kill you. Do you understand?"

"Yes."

"Okay," Callie says. "Come." She holds her arms out. Gwen's face breaks into a broad grin as she moves across the room toward Callie. I see what's about to happen, and jump between them.

Callie arches an eyebrow, which is never a good sign. Word of advice: you ever see Callie Carpenter arch an eyebrow at you, run!

"What the hell's the matter with you?" Gwen says.

"Sorry, I slipped."

"Bullshit!"

Gwen tries to get around me to hug Callie. I mirror her

103

movements, keeping my body between them.

"Do you *mind*?" she says.

"Sorry. I seem to be all tangled up."

I catch Callie's eye. She says, "Creed. Relax."

I move away, and Gwen embraces her. Callie watches me over Gwen's shoulder, completely oblivious to Gwen's affection. I'd come between them just now for a reason. Callie was about to give Gwen a "loving sister," a move I created years ago to be used on my ex-wife, Janet. It works like this: if Janet shoots me and claims self-defense, Callie will meet her a few days after the funeral, and put her arms out as if to give Janet a sisterly hug. Janet will move toward Callie to return the hug, but at the last second, Callie will sidestep her, spin around, come up behind her, and break her neck.

Callie says, "I don't tolerate infidelity. Could it be I didn't make that clear enough to you when killing Eva in your bedroom?"

"She'll be faithful," I say.

"I will!" Gwen says. "I swear!"

"She was willing to have me killed to remove the temptation," I remind Callie.

"That idea might still have legs," Callie says, backing out of Gwen's embrace.

"I'm stepping out. You have my word."

"I don't want you involved with Ropic Industries."

"Good. Because Tony and I haven't been getting along."

"Tony?"

"Tony Spumoni. I think he's planning to file assault charges against me."

Gwen sticks her bottom lip out. "What about my T-shirt company?"

"I'll have them buy you out."

"How much?"

"The company's worth eight million, but they're short on cash and this would be a fire sale."

"How much?"

"Eight hundred thousand."

"Ten percent? That's a terrible deal!"

"It's enough for a T-shirt company."

"Take it," Callie says.

Without batting an eye, Gwen says, "Okay."

I notice she's looking at Callie with bedroom eyes.

"Are we good here?" I say to Callie.

"You and me?"

"Yeah."

"For now."

27.

Maybe Taylor

MAYBE'S FIRST ENCOUNTER with this stupid vaginal muscle spasm thing occurred eighteen months ago. She kept it to herself for a long time, hoping it would go away, but it just got worse. One night, while feeling particularly low, she tearfully explained her problems to Daddy, the man she now calls Ralph. Over time, he talked her into seeing an OBGYN, which is how she obtained the diagnosis. She then met with a specialist, but that didn't work out, so Daddy did an exhaustive search that ended with his paying Dr. Scott a ridiculous amount of money to get Maybe on his patient list.

Over the past few months of therapy, Dr. Scott explored the possible psychological reasons for Maybe's condition, including the fear of painful sex, and the belief that sex is wrong, or dirty. He even suggested a traumatic incident may have triggered her condition. Maybe cooperated in general, but never told Dr. Scott about Taylor, the young man whose name she added to her alias.

Taylor, a wealthy, good-looking kid, had attended J-State. Had a popular girlfriend, Nancy, and dated Maybe on the sly. Taylor's dad was a famous TV personality in Atlanta, his mom a local celebrity. Since his best friend was Nancy's brother, his relationship with Maybe remained a secret.

Taylor and Maybe were on their third date at his parent's lake house in south Georgia. It was November, and the temperature well past chilly. The plan had been to spend a couple of quiet hours there, as they'd done twice before, only this time Maybe promised to go "all the way."

When they arrived that night, the key was missing from its hiding place.

"It's okay," she said. "We can do it in the car."

"I want our first time to be special, in a proper bed," he said. "Wait here."

With that, he went behind the house and broke a small windowpane in the door that led to the den, reached his hand in, and unlocked it. Instead of waiting out front, Maybe followed him inside. Within seconds their clothes were in a heap on the floor, and Taylor, nude except for his socks, chased a naked Maybe down the hall toward the kitchen. Moments later they were on the kitchen floor (so much for a proper bed) and both were benefiting from his extensive sexual experience. After a few minutes he asked Maybe to get on top, and she obliged.

Then all hell broke loose.

Something inside her—a sort of muscle spasm occurred, causing her vagina to clamp down on Taylor's penis. He yelped in pain.

"What are you *doing*?" he yelled.

"*Nothing*! It hurts me, *too*!" she yelled back.

As his erection quickly died, his level of pain increased. Now he was yelling, begging her to call 911.

"My cell phone's on the counter!" she said, through clenched teeth.

"*Do* something!" he screamed.

She tried to stand up, but couldn't. She reached her hand

onto the counter and knocked over what felt like a knife block. She reached up again, and swept the counter. Four objects fell to the floor: his car keys, her cell phone, and two steak knives. Her first thought was Taylor could've been seriously hurt, had the knives fallen the wrong way. Her second thought was she had no intention of allowing police or firemen to catch her in this situation, becoming the object of ridicule, looking for all the world like two dogs caught in mid-fuck. How would they separate them? Pour a pail of water on their crotches? What if one of the rescuers secretly videoed them on his cell phone and put it on the internet?

Taylor kept screaming, "*Call* them! Call *911*!"

Maybe suddenly didn't care for his tone. Or his lack of concern for what would happen when the rescuers arrived. She began to think of Taylor as being weak. After all, she was in pain too. Excruciating pain. But you didn't see *her* freaking out about it. Where was his concern for *her*? She looked down at his face. He was crying. *Crying! What a wimp*, she thought. Maybe grabbed a steak knife in each hand and began stabbing him wherever she could find an opening.

It took much longer than you'd think, but eventually he stopped screaming and flailing and—here's the interesting part—the minute she knew he was dead, her spasm abruptly stopped. She pushed him out of her, used some paper towels, liquid soap, and hot water to wash the blood off her hands and feet. Then she put Taylor's socks on and padded to the guest bedroom, where she took a long, hot shower and scrubbed herself until she was convinced all the blood was gone. Then she walked back to the kitchen, avoiding the blood spots.

She gathered her clothes from the den, dressed, and began the process of wiping down all surfaces she may have touched that night and the other times she'd been there.

Then she got a mop and bucket, some hot water, and cleaned up any traces of her footprints and palm prints. She washed the steak knives carefully, along with Taylor's car keys and her cell phone. Then she locked the door behind her, got in his car, and drove it to a movie theater in Jacksonville, wiped down all the interior surfaces and the outer door handles, then wedged the car keys under the back tire of an SUV on the other side of the parking lot so they'd be crushed when the vehicle backed out of the parking space. From there she walked a mile to her dorm and climbed into bed. Moments later her roommate, Janice, came in, asked how long she'd been there. Maybe said about an hour. She listened with enthusiasm while Janice shared all the details of her date, then they turned off the lights and Maybe slept until ten o'clock the next morning.

28.

Two Days Ago...

MAYBE FINDS HERSELF distracted by thoughts of Daddy. She likes the idea of calling him Ralph, even though she came up with the name to tease him. But if their current relationship turns romantic, and if she's able to open up to him, *literally*, she's not about to call him *Daddy*. Maybe Ralph will eventually tell her his real name.

She has a high profile target this time, a big city mayor. Ralph didn't say which one, and Maybe didn't ask. The mayor and his family are vacationing at a beach condo in Charleston, South Carolina, and all she's been given is the condo address and a key to cubby 17 in the lady's locker room at Oceanwood Country Club.

That's where the gun and silencer will be located, in a large tote bag, suitable for carrying beach items.

Maybe wonders how Ralph obtains weapons and poisons. Once he has them, how does he hide them in places like women's locker rooms? She wonders if he has a team working for him, a team that includes a woman among its members.

Is she jealous?

Maybe thinks about it. She'd like to be part of a team, part of Ralph's close circle of friends. Perhaps even...

What, she thinks. *Marry him and run the team together?*

She laughs. Tells herself to get a grip.

It's four in the afternoon when she strolls through the country club lobby. She enters the women's locker room, sees a number of women milling about. Some are primping in the mirrors in the lounge, others are sitting on benches, in front of open lockers. Maybe doesn't know where cubby 17 is, and doesn't want to be caught perusing the lockers. She's a stranger, and would surely be reported.

"May I help you?" the attendant says, brightly.

"Hi," Maybe says. "Just wanted to use the restroom."

"Of course. Are you showering?"

"I beg your pardon?"

"If you're showering, I'll lay out a fresh towel for you."

"No, I'm fine. Thank you."

The attendant leaves and a voice behind her whispers, "You should be proud of yourself."

Maybe turns. "Excuse me?"

The lady behind her is early thirties. Her hair and makeup perfect. She's smiling, waiting for the attendant to get out of earshot. "I'm Hailey."

Maybe isn't sure what to do or say. "What a coincidence!" she finally says. "That's my name, too!"

Hailey smiles. "No it isn't, but that was a nice recovery. Come."

Maybe follows Hailey into the second row of lockers. They sit together on the bench in front of locker 17. "I'm working with you on this one."

Maybe glances at the locker. Then looks at Hailey.

"Excuse me?" she says. "Working with me on what, my golf game?"

"I'm going to help you kill the mayor," Hailey whispers.

She has her own key, and uses it to open the locker. She

111

removes the tote bag, hands it to Maybe and says, "Let's go out together."

Maybe pauses. "Ralph didn't mention you."

"Who?"

"Daddy."

Hailey looks confused. "Who's *Daddy*?"

"The guy. The one who set this up."

"Oh. Well, it was last minute." She looks around. "Let's not talk here."

"Where, then?"

"Parking lot."

"I don't know if I can trust you."

Hailey laughs. "You're the one with the gun."

They walk out together.

In the parking lot, Maybe says, "Why does he think I'll need help?"

"We just learned the mayor is sharing the condo with two aides and three hookers."

29.

"WHAT DO YOU know about me?" Maybe says.

"I know you're moving up the ladder quickly," Hailey says. "Then again, this is pretty new for all of us."

"I mean, what's he said?"

"About what?"

"Me. What has he told you about me?"

Hailey says, "You want to eat first, or get this done?"

"Excuse me? You mean do it right now?"

"No time like the present. Let's take my car. I've already scoped the place out."

Maybe retrieves her small suitcase from the trunk of her car, and climbs into the passenger seat of Hailey's rental. Hailey guides the car out the parking lot, and down the winding road that leads to a two-lane highway.

"It's a short ride," Hailey says. "Ten minutes, tops. I'll pass by a few times so we can get a feel for how much activity is going on around the unit."

"You plan to do it right now?" Maybe says for the second time.

"Of course. Why? What was your plan?"

Maybe feels a bit foolish, but says, "I figured to take a couple of days. Scope the place out, try to catch the mayor alone, or isolate him from his wife."

"That would've worked," Hailey says, "if the mayor was your only target."

"But now it's the three men?"

"And their whores."

Maybe gives her a look. "The women too?"

"You were *always* supposed to kill the Mayor's wife. He didn't tell you? Jesus. Must've been afraid you wouldn't show up."

Maybe's face turns red. "I would have shown up."

Hailey looks at her. "Maybe, maybe not," she says, then laughs at her joke about Maybe's name.

Maybe says nothing.

Hailey says, "Let me guess: you've never killed a woman before."

Maybe says nothing.

"Are you going to freeze up on me?" Hailey says. "I need to know. Hello? Can you speak to me, please? I mean, we *are* planning a high-profile hit together."

Maybe says, "Are you dating him?"

"*What*? Oh." She smiles. "You're jealous!"

"No, of course not."

"Sounds like it."

"Whatever."

"*Whatever*!" Hailey says, mimicking her.

She drives quietly a couple minutes, then glances over at Maybe and says, "Look, I'm sorry. I'm being a jerk. Truth is I don't know much more than you. I'm all keyed up because…I hate killing innocent people, especially women. He *knows* that."

"How old are they?"

"The women? Well, it's not like they're children, thank God. They're older than you."

Maybe says, "Women, children...it wouldn't matter to me."

Hailey studies her face. "Are you serious? Because I could never kill children. And he better never ask me to!"

Maybe says, "You're too pretty to have been treated badly in high school."

"Excuse me?"

"If there were high school kids here, it wouldn't be hard for me to kill them. I'd just remember the ones who treated me badly in school. I'd think of them, and shoot these."

"You could do that?"

"Sure."

"What about grade school kids?" Hailey says.

"What about them?

"Could you shoot a kid?"

"Yes."

Hailey gives her a look. "How?"

"What do you mean?"

"Jesus!" Hailey says.

30.

AFTER PASSING THE condo twice, Hailey drives all the way to the public beach parking area, a full mile east of the condo.

She says, "We should probably change into bathing suits and cover-ups."

"Right."

"You don't happen to have a large sun hat in your suitcase, do you?"

"I've got a ball cap and sunglasses."

"That'll do."

They get out and head to the public bathroom, change into their suits, and put their clothes in their totes to further conceal their weapons. Maybe puts a second clip into the back pocket of her jeans.

"Is your silencer attached?" Hailey says.

Maybe nods.

The two assassins make their way toward the water, careful to step around the real estate sunbathers have staked out and claimed as their own for the day. Maybe doesn't understand why so many people are sporting angry sunburns. At some point, they've got to know their skin's on fire.

When they get to the hard-packed sand, she says, "What's our boss's name?"

"He should be the one to tell you that."

They walk in silence a few minutes. Then Maybe says,

"Have you slept with him?"

Hailey stops. "Look, honey. You need to take a step back. Not because it's none of your business, but because I can tell he's really got a hold on you. You can't let a man get hold of your mind like that. My ex did that to me, and it was hell on wheels."

"Is that a yes?"

Hailey sighs. "It's a no. I've only met him once."

"When was that?"

"About six weeks ago."

"You've only been doing this for six weeks?"

"No. I was hired and trained by someone else to do this type of work, but he retired about six weeks ago, and passed me off to your boss. I insisted on meeting him."

"What's he like?"

"I can't go into any details. But I can tell you he hates the fact I know his name. Not that I'd ever use it against him. To be honest, I'm not sure I'm cut out for this. I thought I was, but…I don't know. This…" she makes a sweeping gesture with her hand to indicate the hit in general, then shakes her head and starts walking again.

"What about it?" Maybe says, catching up.

"It's not what I signed up for."

"What did you sign up for?"

"Snuffing business men."

"Why?"

Hailey says, "Why am I doing it, or why does he pay me to?"

"The second one."

"I think these guys pose as hit men and hire you and me to do the jobs they're supposed to do. In my case, they used to get all the information on a businessman who's supposed to be killed. When the guy would go out of town to a meeting or convention, I'd get him to lure me to his room. I was married to a serial cheater once. Would've killed him if I could, so I figure these men have it coming. I get paid very well to punish them."

"What if a guy doesn't invite you to his room?"

"That's happened only once out of four times. But you solved that problem."

Maybe thinks a minute. "The college professor?"

"Yup."

"That was my first paying job."

"You're welcome."

"So," Maybe says. "There are just two of us working?"

"Far as I know."

Maybe stops. Hailey says, "What?"

"We're here."

31.

"WHAT'S THE PLAN?" Maybe says. "Walk in, start shooting?"

"You think it might be that simple?"

Maybe checks her watch. "It's after five. They're in the condo, having a fuck fest. Probably celebrating some shady deal. The women are taking showers now, getting ready to go out to dinner. The men are sitting around, drinking a beer. The front and back doors will be unlocked."

"What makes you think that?"

"Six people in the house? Three separate couples? They won't lock the doors till they leave for dinner."

"If they leave."

"Right. If they're cooking tonight, it'll be the men grilling. Either way, the women are showering. We can take them out last."

"Should we go in together?"

"We'll check the doors first. If they're both unlocked, I'll go in the front, which is the second floor, and you can go in the back, the walkout. I'll kill whoever's on the main floor. By then you'll be up the stairs. I'll go to the third floor, and you can cover me." Maybe sees Hailey staring at her.

"What?"

"You sound like you've been doing this all your life."

"Feels like it, too. Ready?"

119

They don't need to test the back door. One of the women is standing next to it, sneaking a cigarette.

"Change of plans," Maybe says. "We'll go in together."

They make a wide arc to the front door. Maybe turns the handle and whispers, "Go left, I'll go right. When we finish this level, go downstairs, shoot the woman. I'll go upstairs and take out the rest, if that's where they are."

Hailey takes a deep breath and nods. She puts her right hand in her tote bag.

"After you," she says.

Maybe opens the door slowly, peeks inside, then enters. Hailey comes in close behind, closes the door, and locks it. Both women remove their guns from their totes, and set the bags down.

32.

MAYBE AND HAILEY are standing in the front hallway. There's a spiral staircase to the right of the front door. From her vantage point, Maybe can see up the staircase, and, leaning over the railing now, can see the stairs below.

In the lower level there's a rumbling noise that sounds like a clothes dryer working overtime. Straight ahead is the empty living room. To the right is the empty kitchen. There appears to be a bedroom off the living room on this floor, and now that Maybe has entered the kitchen, she sees there's a dining room on the other side of it that faces the ocean. The dining room has a sliding glass door that leads to a deck. The door is open, but there's a screen door to keep the bugs out. On the deck is a table with four chairs. Two men are sitting at the table, facing the ocean. They're smoking cigars. Maybe slowly walks to the screen door and shoots them both in the back of the head.

Neither of them falls down. The table appears to be holding them up, though they're slouching against it. Maybe turns to Hailey and motions her to go downstairs. She does. When Maybe turns back, one of the men starts sliding sideways, and falls to the floor. His chair overturns and makes a loud, crashing noise.

The woman sneaking a cigarette directly below the deck, out of view, calls up to ask if everything's okay. Getting no

121

response, she takes several steps toward the beach, turns and looks back onto the deck. At that moment, one of the men raises his hand. The woman comes running inside, yelling, and Maybe can only hope Hailey is standing ready to shoot her. She opens the screen and carefully places another bullet into each man's head. Back in the condo now, the house is quiet, which means Hailey did her part.

Maybe heads toward the master bedroom, turns the door handle, hears a shower running. She enters the bathroom, pulls the glass shower door open, and shoots a heavily tattooed woman—shit!—in the arm. She turned just as Maybe shot. Now she's screaming bloody murder. Maybe fires a second shot right into the center of her mouth. The force of the shot slams her against the back of the shower, and she crashes to the floor, moaning loudly. Maybe puts one more in her temple, then heads back to the staircase. She hears someone coming up the steps.

Hailey.

Maybe motions her to stand guard, and quickly makes her way up the steps. When she gets to the top, there's a landing with yet another deck. Horrified, Maybe realizes this deck overlooks the one below it. If someone had been on it, they would've seen the men get shot. Maybe and Hailey checked the back of the condo earlier, but from their angle, this deck hadn't been visible. It's a lesson learned, and lucky for Maybe, no one was there. She makes a mental note to circle the entire house the next time she finds herself in this situation.

Off the landing there's a door that almost certainly leads to a second master bedroom. Maybe tests the door. It's locked.

On TV and in the movies, this is the part where the hero kicks the door open. Maybe knows you're supposed to aim just left of the door knob. She lifts her foot, then pauses. If she kicks and it doesn't open, whoever's inside will hear.

She lowers her foot, and knocks on the door.

A man's voice says, "Yes?"

Maybe assumes the most adult voice she can, and says, "I'm the owner of this condo. Can I ask what you're doing here?"

"Excuse me?"

"You're not supposed to be here this week."

"Just a minute," the man says. "I'm not dressed.

"I'll wait."

When he opens the door Maybe blows him away before realizing how young he is.

Was.

Twenty-two? Something like that. Obviously one of the aides.

Her eyes dart around the room, seeking the last hooker. She glances once more at the corpse and smiles, remembering how the bullet's impact lifted him off his feet a few seconds ago. One minute he's full of life. The next, he's on the floor, a crimson stain spreading across his chest.

Maybe enters the bedroom, sees clothes strewn all over the place. She enters the bathroom.

No one in the tub.

Separate shower. Opens the door.

No one in the shower.

Toilet door closed. She knocks.

"I'm still in here," a woman's voice says. "Be right out!"

Maybe walks over to the shower and gets the water running, so the woman will think her friend is taking a shower.

Maybe exits the bathroom, walks through the bedroom, steps over the dead guy's body, walks half-way down the stairs and whispers to Hailey, "Did you lock the lower level door?"

Hailey whispers, "Yes. What's going on?"

"Last woman's using the toilet."

"What should we do?"

"Search the men for wallets so we can make a positive ID. I'll go back upstairs and wait."

She goes back into the bathroom and removes the extra clip from her back pocket, sits on the floor, her gun aimed just above the door knob...

Wondering how many bullets she's fired.

She does a mental count.

Eight.

Her weapon holds nine.

Should she replace the clip?

No. Having just one bullet intensifies the high.

Finally, the toilet flushes. A moment later, the woman comes out, does a double-take as she sees Maybe shooting at her, but falls dead before her brain can process what she's seen.

Maybe ejects the clip, replaces it, and heads down the stairs. Hailey's waiting for her, proudly waving the two wallets in the air.

"It's the mayor!" she says.

"Cool," Maybe says. She shoots Hailey in the throat. Hailey's gun clatters as it hits the ceramic tile. Her hands instinctively go to her throat as she staggers a few steps, spewing blood.

"Oops!" Maybe says.

Hailey hits the floor like she'd been dropped from a high place.

"Wh-why?" she whispers.

"You were right. I *was* jealous!"

"H-help me!" Hailey whispers. Her throat is flooded with

blood. It's oozing through her fingers, spilling down her chest.

"I'll help you," Maybe says, "if you tell me his name."

Hailey tries to say something, but her words are garbled.

"You'll have to do better."

Hailey gathers all her strength, tries to shout. Her words come out in a loud, raspy whisper, but they're clear.

The name Maybe hears means nothing to her. And why should it? She doesn't know anyone outside her little circle of acquaintances. She repeats the name to Hailey.

"Sam Case?"

Hailey nods. Then whispers, "P-please h-help me."

Maybe puts one in Hailey's forehead to end her suffering. Then she picks up Hailey's gun, removes the silencer, and drops both pieces into her tote. She repeats the process with her own gun. Then she picks up Hailey's tote bag and removes Hailey's wallet and car keys before stuffing the rest of Hailey's gear, and the bag, into her own tote.

Then she walks out the front door and heads down the two-lane highway all the way to the public beach where Hailey's car is parked. Once there, she drives to the country club, puts the totes and her suitcase in the trunk of her rental car, then drives Hailey's car to a convenience store. She buys the type of wet wipes that contain bleach, uses half of them to remove fingerprints and DNA residue from the interior and exterior of Hailey's car. Then she drives to the airport and turns it over to the guy at the rental car agency, being sure to wipe the steering wheel, gear shift, interior door handle, and the keys with a wet wipe before climbing out.

She walks into the airport, takes the escalator up two floors, and hails a cab to take her back to the country club to retrieve her own car. Before returning it, she goes through the same procedure of wiping down all the surfaces. After returning her rental car, she walks to the airport's long-term parking garage, climbs into her own car, and drives back to Jacksonville.

On the way, she calls Sam Case.

33.

"HI, IT'S ME," Maybe says to the voice mail recorder. "Call when you can."

She's passing the Brunswick exit when his call comes in.

"Everything okay?" he says.

"Peachy."

"Excuse me?"

"I'm still in Georgia. Everything's peachy, get it?"

"Right. Does this mean you finished the job?"

"It does."

"Damn, you're good."

"I know."

"Everything go okay with Hailey?"

"You never said I had to work with someone else."

"Couldn't be helped. Pay's the same, though."

"She froze."

"What?"

"She froze up on me. Killed one of the hookers, and then just stood there. I couldn't get her to leave."

"I don't understand."

"She was catatonic, Sam."

Maybe smiles as it registers in his brain that she used his actual name.

"She told you my name?"

"Yes. Just before she froze."

"She told you my fucking *name*?"

"She did."

"Where is she now?"

"Back at the condo."

"*What*? You *left* her there?"

"Like I said, she was catatonic. There was nothing I could do."

Sam's beginning to panic, and his voice shows it. "You should've killed her!"

Maybe says nothing. Finally Sam says, "You did, didn't you." More like an answer than a question.

"I asked myself, 'what would Sam Case do?' And then yes, I killed her. Didn't want to, but I was afraid she might tell the authorities what she knew. Did I do good?"

He pauses. "You're telling me the truth?"

"You don't *believe* me?"

"I didn't say that. It's just, I don't understand why she'd freeze up like that."

"On the way there she said she couldn't deal with killing innocent people. Said you hired her to kill businessmen, and she didn't sign up for this type of work."

"You got all that out of her? Plus my name?"

"I don't know how you ever trusted her. I can't believe you slept with her."

"What?"

"She told me all about it."

"That's not true."

"You're denying it?"

"If she said that, she was lying. I met her exactly once in person."

"How can I believe you? Sounds like everything else she said was true. I don't know why she'd lie about that."

128

"Are you okay?"

"I don't know. Depends on if I can trust you."

"I'm telling the truth. Hailey and I never had sex. Period."

"That's your story and you're sticking to it."

"It is, and I am. And it's the truth."

"So you say."

They're both quiet a minute. Sam ends the silence.

"Guess we're lucky she got one of them. Did you verify it was the mayor?"

"Yes."

"I hate to lose Hailey, but it's clear you've become my go-to person."

"I'm glad you feel that way, seeing as it was just the two of us anyway."

"I'm going to ask you a question," Sam says. "I know the answer, but I have to ask."

"Go ahead."

"What happened to her car, her luggage, and so forth?"

Maybe tells him.

"You're a natural," Sam says.

"My turn to ask a question."

"Okay."

"Is your name really Sam Case?"

"Yes."

"Why's that a big deal?"

"Who said it was?"

"If it's not a big deal, why haven't you told me? You say you love me, want to have sex with me, want me to trust you, but you won't tell me your name?"

"You call yourself Maybe. Because you may or may not stay."

"I think you and Hailey had a thing. You told her your name."

"Let's move beyond this silliness. I want you, and I can tell you're ready to be with me."

"You're pretty cocky."

"And you're pretty."

"Are we going to meet?" Maybe says.

"Yes."

"When?"

"Soon."

"Are you married?"

He pauses. "Yes."

Maybe pauses. Then says, "Have you told your wife you want to fuck me?"

"No. But she's got a lover. We've lived apart for a long time. She's actually trying to get pregnant, and not with me."

"Bummer."

"Is that all you've got to say?"

"No. I want you to pay me the balance you owe me, and the balance you owe Hailey."

"What right do you have to her share?"

"I saved your bacon today. You were going to pay her anyway."

"Okay," Sam says.

"Okay?"

"It's reasonable. Anything else?"

"Yes. I want you to bring the money in person."

Sam thinks a minute. "How about tomorrow night, seven o'clock?"

"Where?"

"Your place."

"Really?"

"Really."

"Are you going to bring your wife?"

"Do you want me to?"

"Not this time."

34.

Present Day...
Donovan Creed.

GEORGE BEST IS furious about meeting me at PhySpa this late at night, but the only other option I offered was his house, with his wife present.

"You'll do well to hold your temper," I say.

"Why? Are you going to rip my ear off if I don't?"

I point to a large item on the table between us. "Ever seen one of these?"

He looks at the industrial staple gun and shrugs. He's not impressed.

I pick it up, stand, lean my weight on it while pressing it to the table top. When I click the trigger, George jumps at the sound. When I move the gun he sees the top of a steel staple resting flush against the table top.

George plays it cool. He puts a little edge in his voice and says, "What's so important it can't wait till tomorrow morning?"

"The bomb that went off at Landmark and Trace?"

"What about it?"

"I was there."

He gives me a look of disdain. "Somehow that doesn't surprise me."

"I was a witness, not a participant."

"So?"

"The bomb was detonated by a guy in a white van."

I'm feeding George a little piece at a time, waiting for him to either fill in the blanks or keep saying "So?"

He says, "So?"

George isn't a tough guy, but he's no pushover, either. Pushovers don't contact arms dealers and mislead them about a weapon's effectiveness.

He's sitting there, angry, arms folded in front of his chest, working hard to keep the anger out of his voice.

"Let's cut to the chase," I say.

He shows me his pissed-off look. Then says, "Why are you smiling?"

I'm smiling because I realize George isn't fighting to hold back his anger. He's trying to hide his fear.

I say, "Tell me the truth. How much trouble are you in?"

Instead of responding, he does something that takes me completely by surprise.

He bursts into tears.

35

GEORGE ISN'T JUST crying, he's sobbing. He buries his head in his arms on the table, convulsing with each sob. It strikes me this could take a while. I check my watch and wonder if I should have eaten something on the way over.

George is sitting directly across from me, but all I see are his arms and the top of his head. He's mid forties, appears to have a nice head of hair. He's wearing a flannel shirt, which makes me wonder how many tears it could absorb if he was sitting up instead of allowing them to leak all over my table. Of course, I can't complain about the table. I just put a flippin' staple in the center of it. I pick up the staple gun and inspect it, take a minute to wonder how far it can shoot, and try to guess whether it would have the ability to penetrate over distance.

George continues to sob.

I wonder what Dr. Phyllis Willis would say if she saw this beautiful table with a staple in it. In truth, I was surprised the staple "took." I'm not a wood expert, but I thought the table top was some sort of laminate. I figured the staple would make a loud sound, maybe crack the laminate or something, but had no idea it would actually penetrate the wood. Seeing George fall apart so easily, I'm starting to think I put a hole in a perfectly good table for nothing. Then again, it felt incredibly satisfying to pull the trigger and see the result. I find myself wanting to put another staple in the table.

George is still sobbing. There's something in his crying that doesn't sound quite right. I focus on the staple in the table, and wonder what the best way would be to remove it.

When George stops crying I look up at him and notice he's pointing a gun at the center of my chest.

Good thing his gun's a semi-automatic. Unless there's a round already in the chamber, he can't just pull the trigger and shoot me. He's got to manually load the first round by racking the slide mechanism.

"Helluva gun you've got there," I say.

"You think?"

"K11 Slovak. You didn't buy that at Walmart. Your arms dealer must've given it to you as a gift."

"That's right."

"I would've held out for a K100 Whisper with a threaded barrel and silencer. Of course I'd never try to use either of these guns."

He frowns. "Why not?"

"Arms dealers are notorious bastards. Your gun is probably rigged to blow up in your face."

"You're not going to trick me into giving up my gun."

"Fine. Let me ask you this: what's your arms dealer's name?"

"Boris."

I chuckle.

"What's so funny?"

"Nothing. Okay, so I'm guessing at some point Boris asked what else you have that might be for sale, right?"

"So?"

"And I'm guessing you said this is all you've got, right?"

George frowns again.

I say, "So we've got an arms dealer using a fake name who's negotiating with a rookie on a one-shot deal. And he gives you a K11 Slovak?" I chuckle again. "Did he provide the ammunition, too?"

George says, "Whatever you're up to, it won't work."

"I'm on your side here, Gumby."

"*My* side? You ripped the ears off my friend. You held us captive in this very room. You're trying to force us to manufacture T-shirts with a stripper! We take our business very seriously, Mr. Creed."

"Then you'll be pleased to know I talked Mrs. Peters into selling her shares back to the company."

"For how much?"

"Eight hundred thousand."

"Bullshit. They're worth at least four times that much."

"Quick sale. Certified check. She'll make T-shirts, you guys do whatever you want."

"You both know too much."

"Thanks for the compliment."

"You know what I mean."

"Of course. Knowing what you mean is a natural extension of knowing too much."

"You're half as funny as you think."

"The eight hundred buys Gwen's shares and her silence."

"What about you?"

"I still want to meet Boris."

"He's threatening to kill my family."

"I figured as much. That's how they roll. Put the gun down, and we'll talk about it."

"No."

I angle the staple gun slightly upward and pull the trigger. The staple hits his hand and makes him lose his grip on the gun. I jump across the table and knock it to the floor. George tries to reach beneath him to pick it up, but before his hand can find it, I've struck him with enough force to knock him out.

Like tearing off an ear, delivering a one-punch knockout blow requires a great deal of technique. The human brain is suspended in liquid, so a blow must be hard enough to force the brain to move through the liquid and strike the interior of the skull. The harder the brain hits the skull, the longer the victim remains unconscious. Boxers aim for the chin for several reasons. One, the mandibular nerve is located behind the hinge of the jaw, and the biomechanical response to a sudden impact is overload. Two, the jaw is the most muscular part of the face, and provides the most cushion for your fist, which allows for greater impact. Three, the chin is the furthest facial point from the brain, and affords your blow the most leverage. It makes the top of the head move faster in the opposite direction of the blow, which in turn causes the brain to pass through the liquid and hit the skull.

When George wakes up he finds himself on his back, on the conference table, unable to move. I've stapled the sleeves and sides of his shirt, and his pants, to the table. There's no pain involved, but he's understandably nervous.

"Wh-what are you going to do?" he says.

"I'm going to stop the terrorists."

"How?"

"I've got a plan, but it requires some answers. Ready?"

"Yes."

36.

"LET'S START WITH the chip they put in Connor Payne's brain."

"What about it?"

"The chip can be activated by punching a four-digit code into a wrist device that looks like a watch."

"That's old news."

"Dr. Willis told the government only two wrist units were manufactured."

"So?"

"Apparently there were five."

"Lucky Peters told you that?"

"Yes."

"And you believe him?"

"I do."

"Why?"

"When a corporation's medical director shares a bed with its largest stockholder, over time, there's a lot more than body fluids being exchanged."

"That's disgusting."

I can already account for three of the devices. My homeland security boss, Darwin, has one. Doc Howard, who placed the chip in my brain, had the second device, but sold it to me for a hundred million bucks. Dr. Phyllis Willis had the third, but I confiscated it after killing her. Which leaves two wrist devices unaccounted for. I think I know where one of them is.

"You sold one of the wrist devices to the arms dealer, correct?"

"Of course. That's the only way to detonate the chips."

"And you've got one."

"Why would you assume that?"

"Because I know how you guys operate."

"Whether we do or don't, what difference does it make? All the chips are gone."

"How many chips did you sell? Hundreds?"

"Two hundred and twelve."

"Any idea where they are now?"

"No."

"That's why I want to meet Boris."

"I still don't understand."

"I assume he's reprogrammed the chips so that each is linked to a specific code."

"Of course. And whoever he sold them to has reprogrammed them again."

"But my ceramic device can reset those codes, correct?"

He looks confused for a minute, then says, "Holy shit!"

I smile.

George says, "Why do you need to talk to Boris?"

"I want to know what he's done with the chips."

"I can tell you what he's done with them. He's sold them to terrorist cells all over the world!"

"You think?"

"I know it for a fact."

"Do you suppose he's like you guys?"

"What do you mean?"

"Two hundred and twelve's an odd number of chips. You think he sold two hundred and kept a dozen for himself?"

George says, "Now that you mention it, I think it's a certainty."

"I think so too. How many chips do you think each terrorist cell has in their stash?"

"Probably twenty groups have ten each."

"Or ten have twenty."

"Or forty have five."

I think about it a minute, and say, "It's more likely fifty terrorist cells have four chips each."

"Why?"

"There are only so many times you can sew bombs into people's mouths in the same neighborhood without attracting attention."

George says, "You don't need to meet Boris! If you've got the ceramic device, we can reprogram everything right now! We can kill Boris and a bunch of terrorists at the same time!"

George is right. I don't need Boris. And I probably *could* kill dozens of terrorists in one fell swoop, assuming they've stashed the chips in their homes, or their clothing. Of course, there will be instances where I'm simply blowing up chips in an empty building or storage locker, or hole in the ground where they've been buried. But there's a high probability key people would be killed, and probably Boris, since twelve chips going off at the same time would kill him if he's anywhere near his stash.

"Do you think Boris knows about the ceramic device?"

"No one knows about it."

"Except you and the board members," I say.

"Right. And Gwen Peters."

"Which means a lot of people could know by now."

"True. We'd better hurry up and change the code."

"I can't do that, George."

"Of course you can! Press the button four times and blow the bastards to hell!"

"I can't."

"Why not?"

"I'm Connor Payne."

He thinks about that.

"You killed Dr. Willis?"

I say nothing.

"And her staff?"

I say nothing.

He goes quiet a minute. Then says, "Are you going to kill me?"

"Probably."

"I've got a family."

"I know. And I've got a problem."

"What problem?"

"As I see it, there are two ways to do this. First, I can plug the ceramic device into the wrist unit, and reprogram each of the two hundred and twelve chips, as well as the chip in my brain."

George says, "That only works if you know the codes in advance."

"In that case, I only have one option. Press the button on the ceramic device four times in ten seconds and blow up all the units at once."

"Correct."

"But when I press the four digits to kill the terrorists, I'll boil my own brains."

"Oh."

"Exactly."

He says, "You have to do it anyway."

"What?"

"You have to sacrifice yourself. This is a chance to save not only my family, but thousands of families all over the world!"

"What kind of man would I be not to do that?" I ask.

"Exactly," George says. "It's a horrible situation, but it's the right thing to do."

"Think on it a little longer. Maybe there's a way to reprogram the other chips while bypassing the one in my head."

My cell phone vibrates. I walk toward the door.

"Where are you going?"

"I've got a call. Work on my problem till I get back."

37.

"BAD NEWS, DONOVAN," Lou says.

"Let's hear it."

"The guy we had tailing Kimberly last year? Jimmy T.?"

"What about him?"

"He's dead."

I pause to let the news sink in. "What happened?"

"He moved to South Carolina, changed his name, got a teaching job at Viceroy College."

"What was his new name?"

"Jonah Toth."

"What happened, heart attack?"

"He was murdered."

"Where?"

"In the men's room. At the college."

"When?"

"That's the weird part. This happened a week ago today."

"Did they get the guy who did it?"

"No leads. No one knows anything. He taught his class, walked across the hall to use the bathroom, got shot standing at the urinal.

"And this happened a week ago."

"A week ago exactly."

"Could he have been on drugs? Fooling around on his wife? Anything like that?"

"Are you asking if he got caught with his dick out?"

"Good one. Since you brought it up, did the report specify?"

"It did. Care to bet?"

"Fifty bucks says it was out."

"Is that your bet?"

"It is."

"I'll pay you next time I see you."

"All jokes aside," I say. "Was he doing something wrong?"

"He was clean and faithful a year ago," Lou says. "But people can change."

"Can you get me someone else to keep an eye on Kimberly? I want to make sure she's safe."

"I'll work on it."

When I enter the consultation room a few minutes later, I'm holding a syringe in my hand.

"How about it George? Got a solution to my problem yet?"

38.

"UIC," GEORGE SAYS.

"What's that?"

"A possible solution for your problem."

"Tell me."

"UIC, the University of Illinois at Chicago, has the strongest Magnetic Resonance Imaging Machine in the world. It's got a 45 ton magnet that generates a 9.4 Tesla magnetic field!"

"Pretend I'm not as smart as you and tell me why that's a big deal."

"Most MRI machines generate 3 Tesla."

"Talk to me, George. I have no idea what you're saying."

"If you can arrange to be scanned by that particular machine for at least twenty minutes, the magnetic field it generates should be powerful enough to erase the data imbedded in the chip."

"*Should* be able to?"

"There are no guarantees, of course, but yes. I'm virtually certain."

"If the machine is that special, there's probably a long waiting list to use it."

"I'm sure. Do you have any government connections?"

I do. My boss, Darwin, could get me in there in minutes. Unfortunately, he's the one who ordered the chip placed in my brain.

"No," I say.

"Then you'd have to wait awhile. But you can't."

"Why's that?"

"Because Boris is going to kill my family."

"You seem like an honest man," I say.

"Thanks."

"You're asking me to sacrifice my life. Would you sacrifice *your* life to save *my* family?"

He pauses. "*Your* family? No. Your family and thousands of others? Yes, absolutely."

"How about *your* family?"

"Of course."

"I believe you."

I press the syringe into his neck. As he starts to die, I say, "You're a good man. I'll make sure your family is safe. You have my word."

I didn't want to kill George, but it was the smart play. Now that he's dead, Boris has nothing to gain by killing George's family. The Las Vegas terror cell will think Boris killed George, which will help appease them. I can de-magnetize the chip *and* kill the terrorists, and live to kill more of them. It's not that I'm *unwilling* to sacrifice myself, I just think I'm more valuable alive than dead.

As I head for the tool box to remove the staplers from the table, I realize I've got another problem. Who do I trust to hold the ceramic device while I'm getting the MRI? I can't take the device in there with me, for fear the magnet will destroy its imprint. Without that, I wouldn't be able to detonate the chips.

I stop to think who I trust enough to safeguard the device for twenty minutes.

Callie could do it, but can I trust her not to press the

button four times while I'm in the imaging room? Until a few weeks ago I would've trusted her completely. But she's made comments recently that make me wonder. I seriously doubt she'd kill me while I'm on the table. Then again, she might.

I could certainly trust Kimberly, if she'll take my call.

I open my cell phone and try.

No answer.

I leave a message: "Kimberly, please call me when you get this message. Anytime before nine a.m. tomorrow morning, eastern time."

If I can get an appointment tomorrow I'll fly Kimberly to Chicago by private jet. She can hold the device for twenty minutes and maybe spend a day or two with me. Maybe we can patch things up between us.

What if she doesn't call back? Who then?

Not Lou Kelly. He tried to kill me once already.

Not Rachel, my girlfriend. She's living in an underground bunker, having her eggs harvested by the government. Plus, she's homicidal.

Not Gwen. She tried to kill me *today*.

Not Janet, the ex-wife. She'd *love* to see me dead.

Not Darwin, my boss. He wants the chip active so he can kill me whenever it suits him.

What about…Beth?

Beth Daniels owns *The Seaside*, a quaint little bed and breakfast in St. Alban's Beach, Florida. She and I never hooked up in the classic sense, but there was some serious chemistry between us during the short time Rachel and I worked for her. We sort of left things in limbo, and I never called her back, figuring she's better off without me. She's the right woman for me, but I'm all wrong for her, which is why I can't ask her to fly to Chicago to safeguard a chip for me.

I would certainly trust Kathleen Gray. Well, her last name isn't Gray anymore, which is one of the two reasons I can't ask *her* to safeguard the chip. The other is she thinks I'm dead. Kathleen's a married woman now, living in New York, and it would completely disrupt her life if I suddenly appeared.

I trust two others: Miranda Rodriguez, and Nadine Crouch. Miranda's my favorite hooker, and Nadine's my former shrink.

It's pitiful to admit the list of friends I can trust is shorter than the list of friends who've tried to kill me.

39.

IF KIMBERLY CALLS me back, she's my first choice. If not, I'll try Miranda. Why Miranda over Nadine? She's non-judgmental, she's beautiful, and she'd love to fly to Chicago to spend a couple of romantic days with me. For a fee. Assuming another client hasn't booked her yet, and that she's not busy with a project at NYU, where she's working toward her Master's in Counseling Psychology.

I decide to call Miranda, to put her in the on-deck position in case Kimberly fails to call. When her voice mail comes on, I leave a message. When I hang up, it dawns on me I left her and Kimberly the same message. It also registers I have three women in my life who are twenty years old. One's my daughter, one's my lover, and the third is Gwen, who tried to have me killed today, after having sex.

I know what you're thinking. I need to get involved with a nice woman my own age, right? Problem is, I don't know any hookers my age.

It's possible neither Kimberly nor Miranda will call me back. And I don't want to fly to Cincinnati to drop the device off with Nadine. It would be in her care for hours instead of minutes. It would make more sense to hire four security guards in Chicago and have them accompany me to UIC. I'd put the device in a locker outside the MRI room and hire one to stand in front of it and the other three to watch him!

Then I realize I don't even have an appointment.

Since I can't trust Darwin, and Dr. Petrovsky's a plastic surgeon, I can only think of one doctor who might be able to get me in.

Dr. Howard.

I dial his number.

"Damn it, Creed! Why is it you never call me during business hours?"

"Because you never take my calls during the day."

"That's bullshit. What do you want?"

"I need an MRI appointment this afternoon at UIC."

"Why?"

I tell him. Turns out he's heard about their jumbo MRI machine.

"Why do you need a scan?"

I tell him that, too.

"I don't have that kind of pull," he says.

"Listen up, Doc. You're the one that put the chip in my head. Then you charged me a hundred million dollars—a hundred *million* dollars!—for the code to deactivate it, and then you tell me I'm still at risk. You *owe* me."

"I *do* owe you. But I don't know how you expect me to get you in. Or what I'm supposed to tell them."

"You're going to tell them it's a national emergency, that I'm an agent with homeland security and I've got a chip in my brain and you need to know if it can be surgically removed. While I'm getting the scan, the magnet should erase the imbedded messaging."

He sighs.

"What's magic about this afternoon?"

"What if I told you I have a chance to kill dozens of terrorists all over the world if I can get this chip deactivated?"

"I'd tell you to call Darwin."

"I can't. He's the one that made you implant the chip. He'd never allow it to be erased."

"Darwin's a lot of things, and many of them are vile. But first and foremost he's a patriot. I bet he'd allow it, if you can convince him there's a connection between erasing the chip and killing a bunch of terrorists."

"I can't trust him. But I'll trust you. I've uncovered an arms deal. Two hundred chips have been distributed to terror cells all over the world. At least one of them is in Las Vegas, and I'm certain there are many more in the US. If I can de-magnetize the chip in my head, I'll be free to reprogram the chip codes and blow them all up at the same time, all over the world. I'm betting dozens of terrorists have the chips in their possession. When I reset the code, they'll blow up."

"And you have a way of resetting the code? Some sort of device?"

"I've said all I'm going to say."

"You need to de-magnetize the chip because when you reset the codes and detonate the chips, the chip in your head will also be activated."

"That's right."

"If you don't get the scan, you're not willing to blow up the other chips."

"Would you?"

"No."

"Then get me the appointment."

"I'll try. But I don't see the urgency about having this done this afternoon."

"The terror cell in Vegas sewed a chip into an illegal alien's mouth yesterday, and blew her head off trying to determine how powerful the explosion would be. Every passing day increases the possibility of a terrorist attack. Thousands of lives are at stake."

"How big a danger are these chips?"

"What do you mean?"

"It seems like the charge would only be powerful enough to kill the person holding it, and possibly a few others."

"You can bet they won't use the chips that way."

"Then how?"

"I expect they'll set plastique in key places and use the chips as detonators, like blasting caps."

"But if you can blow them up while they're holding them—"

"Exactly."

"So what's this device that can be used to reprogram the chips?"

"That's not something you need to worry about."

"The reason I'm asking, you won't be able to have it anywhere near the imaging room, correct?"

"That's right."

Doc Howard pauses. Then says, "I'll do what I can."

40.

Present Day...
Maybe Taylor.

MAYBE SCREAMS OUT in pain, instinctively moves her hand to her crotch, realizes she's still wearing her jeans. Opens her eyes. Her head's in a fog. "What time is it?"

"Two a.m.," Sam says.

"What did you *do* to me just now?"

"Nothing. You were dreaming."

"What's happened?"

"I came to your place at seven last night. The first thing you said was you hoped I'd be better looking."

Maybe yawns. "That's true. And *you* said I was good looking enough for both of us."

"Right. Then I took you to dinner."

"Then we went to a hotel."

"We're still at the hotel."

"Why's it so dark in here?"

"It's the middle of the night. What else do you remember?"

"I remember telling you there would be no sex."

"That was three hours ago."

"Then what happened?"

"We had a drink, and I gave you something to help you relax."

"You didn't try to fuck me, did you?"

"No."

"Good," Maybe says.

"Why's that good?"

"Because you're too old for me. And creepy."

"That's just a first impression."

"What time is it?" she says.

"3:30."

"I thought you said two."

"That was ninety minutes ago."

"Are we still in the hotel room?"

"Yes."

The next time Maybe opens her eyes the lights are on. "Sam?"

"I'm right here, beside you. It's four-twelve."

She's lying down on a bed. Her head is still fuzzy, but something feels strange "down there." What's strange is she feels numb. She props herself up on her elbows, sees she's naked from the waist down. A dildo is protruding from between her legs.

"What the *fuck*?"

"Surprise!" Sam says.

She launches a fist toward his face and nearly breaks his nose.

He yelps, but moves in closer and says, "Hit me as much as you want, as hard as you want, for as long as you want. My only wish is for you to be happy."

She slaps his face. Looks at him, says, "What's the *matter* with you?" Then slaps him again.

"I want you to have a normal life, free of pain."

She slaps him again. "You *bastard*! You had no right to touch me!"

154

He removes the pillow case from a pillow, dabs the blood from his nose and corner of his mouth, looks at it, dabs again. Then says, "Slap me if you want, but realize for the first time in more than a year, you're not in pain."

Maybe raises her arm to hit him again, then stops. Looks down. The dildo isn't as large as the giant purple one Dr. Scott had on his tray, but it's larger than any of the three young men who've spent time inside her. She reaches down and slides it out, noting the complete lack of pain. She briefly touches herself where the dildo had been, wonders if she's dreaming. Then realizes if she's *not* dreaming, she's naked in real life! She pulls a sheet over herself, and goes back to sleep.

41.

4:15 a.m., Pacific Daylight Time.
Donovan Creed.

I DON'T REQUIRE a nice bed or fancy sheets. While at PhySpa, I grab a pillow from the lobby couch, toss it on one of the office floors, and lay my head wherever it lands. No sheets, no bed, no problem. I put my cell phone charger wherever there's a nearby outlet, and find something made of wood or plastic to set it on so the vibration will make a rattling sound when someone calls.

Like it's doing right now.

As I reach for it, I play a three-second game of trying to decide who's calling at seven-fifteen a.m., Eastern Time. My guess is Miranda. She probably just got in from a "date" and found the message light on. I can picture her exhausted, trying to force a happy voice for my benefit.

I'm wrong. It's Doc Howard.

"Five-forty this afternoon," he says, "Central time. It's the best I can do."

"How on earth?"

"I won't *begin* to tell you how much trouble I went through to make this happen. Let's just say you owe me."

"Thanks, Doc."

"Get there thirty minutes early, to check in."

"You got an address?"

"No!"

He hangs up.

Thanks to Doc Howard, I've got an appointment. But I'm still left with the problem of finding someone to safeguard the device while I'm in the imaging room. While I *generally* trust Doc Howard, he might feel compelled to tell Darwin my plans, since they involve the unauthorized killing of terrorists. He also might tell in order to cover his ass. Doc Howard planted the chip under Darwin's orders, so it makes sense he'd tell Darwin I asked him to set an appointment to have the chip erased.

I think a minute. Would he tell Darwin before or after making the appointment?

Before.

Not saying he told Darwin anything, but if he did, he would've told him I know about the chip, and that I'm planning to have it erased. If Darwin told him to set the appointment, he might have decided this is his last, best chance to kill me, since he knows exactly where I'll be at five-forty. Worse, I'll be vulnerable for at least twenty minutes while I'm being scanned in the imaging room. From five-forty to six p.m. I'll be unarmed, completely immobilized, on my back, with my head in the machine.

I'll be as helpless as Curly, after Moe and Larry stick his head in a vice.

I press the button to call Jeff Tuck.

"You asleep?"

"I was dreaming of tea and crumpets with the Queen."

"Is Joe with you?"

"He's on the desk." Meaning he's watching the bank of TV monitors to ensure nobody's sneaking up on us.

157

"I'll meet you there."

"Do I have time to piss?"

"You do."

Moments later, the three of us are in the security room.

"I need you guys to come with me to Chicago."

"When?" Joe says.

"Now."

"What about George?"

"How long's he been in the freezer?"

"Not even close."

I sigh. The plan is to freeze him solid, lift the freezer lid, and cut him into chunks right where he is, to keep the blood contained. Then we'll put the chunks in plastic bags, place the plastic bags in laundry bags, and carry them to our cars, and scatter the pieces in various parts of the desert.

"We can't leave George unguarded," Jeff says.

"I agree. Joe, you stay. Jeff will go with me."

"How much should I pack?" Jeff says.

"We'll be back tonight."

"Give me two minutes."

I tell Joe to keep an eye on things.

He nods.

I call Lou. When he answers, I say, "You'll be pleased to know I've got a job for you."

"What's that?"

"I need a jet."

"Where and when?"

"I need to land in Chicago at four, local time."

"Today?"

"Yeah."

"You'll need to leave by ten."

"That'll work."

158

I hang up and immediately call my friends at Koltech Aviation in Las Vegas. Bob Koltech answers.

"I'll pay you sixty grand to fly me to Chicago and back."

"When do you want to leave?"

"Right now."

"Are you here at the gate?"

"No, but I can be there in fifteen minutes."

"Which jet do you want?"

I notice another call coming in. I say, "The fastest one you've got."

"I'll have her warmed up and ready to roll when you get here."

"Good man."

I click him off and click the next caller through.

Miranda.

"I'm so glad to hear from you!" she says. "Seems like a million years!"

"Me too," I say.

"What's up?"

"I planned to fly you to Chicago to meet me around noon, Central Time, but my plans have changed. I'm heading there now. I appreciate you calling, but it's not going to work at this point."

"Whoa, cowboy. You can't get rid of me that easily. I'd love to meet you! Please? I'll put a huge smile on your face!"

"I could use a huge smile."

"I can be there by eleven. Maybe we can have lunch, spend the day together. And the night, if you'd like."

"I'd love it, but—"

"Then it's set. I know you're busy, so I'll book my own flight. Where are we staying?"

"I don't have a room. I was planning to head back to Vegas

later today."

"No problem. I'll text you my itinerary, and call when I get there. If we don't connect, I'll shop till I hear from you."

She makes a great case for staying in Chicago.

"Sounds great. Thanks, Miranda."

"No," she says. "Thank *you*!"

After hanging up I head to the kitchen, look in the closet where Phyllis kept the party supplies from when she had birthday parties for her employees. Amid the gift paper, bags, tissue, and such, I pick a small box, place the ceramic device in it, gift wrap it, and stuff it in my pocket. Then I go to my safe and remove a suitcase that holds one hundred twenty thousand dollars in hundreds, and five thousand in twenties. Then Jeff and I head to the private airfield where Bob Koltech has our jet waiting.

Normally I trust Lou to book my flights. But on the chance Darwin knows what I'm up to, he'll get my itinerary from Lou. If Lou thinks I'm leaving Vegas at ten, Darwin will think so, too.

I do lead a complicated life.

42.

Maybe Taylor

"HOW'D YOU DO it?" Maybe asks.

"You mean, why didn't it hurt when I inserted the dilator?" Sam says.

"Yeah."

"I injected you with Botox."

"*What*?"

"It's a little tricky, and I had to study up on it. The whole purpose is to relax the muscle spasm."

"That's the pain I felt in the middle of the night."

"Yes."

"But I had my jeans on. I felt them!"

"Your jeans were on top of your legs."

"You're an asshole."

Sam sighs. "The point of botox therapy is for you to wake up after achieving the hardest part, which is the insertion of a large dilator. When you see it inside you, as you did, your brain begins to understand this is something you can do. So that's the first step."

"What's the second?"

"Training your vaginal muscles to respond to the dilator over time."

"How much time?"

"Hard to say. Months, certainly."

"It obviously happened that once," Maybe says. "But it couldn't happen again. You don't understand. No one does."

Sam starts to pull the sheet off her. She grabs it and says, "What the hell are you doing?"

"Check it out," he says, giving up his grip on the sheet.

She lifts the sheet and peeks beneath it. To her astonishment, the dildo is back where it was earlier.

"Keep your fucking hands off my snatch!" she says.

Sam assumes a defensive posture, with his hands up, guarding his face. He says, "I love you."

"You're a degenerate. I never gave you permission to sexually violate me."

"I know you don't find me attractive," Sam says.

"No shit! And it's not just a matter of looks. You've got the whole 'call me Daddy' thing going on, and you're way older than me, which makes it twice as creepy. You've made me a kept woman, paying for all these lessons and whatnot, and now you're trying to collect a sexual payment for it."

"I won't argue with anything you said. But whether you believe or not, I'm a good guy. I'm incredibly smart, talented in many ways that can benefit you, and I love you. I'd do anything for you. Do you believe that?"

"No."

"Put me to the test."

"You'd fail."

"Try me."

"Fine. Leave your wife."

"Are you asking me if I'd get a divorce?"

"Yes."

"Are you offering me anything in return? Anything at all?"

"No."

"The answer's yes. If you want me to, I'll divorce her immediately."

"Call her."

"What, right now?"

"Yes. With me listening."

"It's seven-fifteen!"

"So?"

"You don't know Rachel."

He shrugs, gets his cell phone, and presses a button.

"Put it on speaker," Maybe says.

He clicks the speaker button.

A woman answers.

"Mmm?"

"Rachel?"

"Huh?"

"It's me, Sam."

"Who?"

"Your husband. Sam."

She yawns. "Where are you?"

"Doesn't matter."

"What do you want? I'm trying to sleep."

"I've found someone else. I want a divorce."

"Is this a joke?"

"No. I'm totally serious."

"Thanks, Sam."

"You're welcome."

The phone goes silent. As he's about to hang up, she says, "Sam?"

"Yeah?"

"I hope she makes you very happy."

"Thanks."

He hangs up.

Maybe says, "She didn't sound too broken up about it."

"She's crying on the inside."

43.

MAYBE LAUGHS. "YOU'RE funny. In a non-comedic sort of way."

"Thanks," Sam says.

"Are you really going through with it?"

"The divorce?"

"Yes."

"I am. Rachel's in love with someone else. I may as well let her get on with her life."

"And you just now decided this?"

"I hadn't considered her feelings till now. I was too angry at her for cheating on me."

Sam puts the phone on the nightstand and lies down beside her on the bed. She hands him the dilator. "I believe this belongs to you."

He puts it in his mouth.

"Eew," she says.

He places it on the night stand and says, "I love you. I've loved you for months."

She's under the sheet, naked from the waist down. He's lying above the covers, fully clothed. They remain quiet a long time before Maybe breaks the silence. "I'm not going to be your girlfriend. You know that, don't you?"

He sighs. "Is it completely impossible for us to have a romantic relationship?"

"Completely."

"What if we were the last two people on Earth?"

"Even then."

"So it's hopeless?"

"Look into my face."

He does.

"I will never love you."

"Can I ask why?"

"There are too many reasons to list. But I want someone special, someone who makes me all giddy and girly. I want to have children someday, and a husband with a normal job."

"You'd be bored shitless."

"Maybe I would, eventually. But it'd be fun to live the fairy tale for as long as it works."

"Trust me, the fairy tale's a myth. That's why they call it a fairy tale."

"See? That's another reason it wouldn't work between us. You're too negative."

"You're right."

"You agree?"

"Yes. But here's the thing."

He pauses.

"I'm listening."

"What if the world's most perfect guy comes along, and you can't perform?"

"Sexually?"

"Yes. What if there's a point in your relationship when you want to give him everything, but you can't, because of the pain, or the fear of pain, whether it's psychological, physiological, or both. I can't think of anything sadder than losing the man of your dreams because you can't give him intimacy."

166

"You can't, huh?"

"I'm being serious."

"What's your point?"

"My point is when Mr. Right enters your life, you need to be ready for him. And what I mean by that is you need to feel comfortable. You need to feel confident about your sexuality, and there's only one way that can be achieved."

"And what way is that?"

"Practice."

Maybe bursts into laughter. Her whole body shakes as her laughter cascades from her throat and bounces off the furniture. Tears start to form in her eyes.

"What is so fucking funny?" Sam says.

"You're the most manipulative bastard I've ever met!" she says, then laughs again.

"I admit it. But that doesn't make me wrong."

"Yes it *does*! That's *exactly* what makes you wrong."

"Think about it," Sam says. "Who could possibly be better to help you get through this? I'm the only man in your life who knows about your sexual issues, and the only person who's managed to get you dilated without pain. I've followed every step of your treatment. I've seen you naked. I've *touched* you."

"Inappropriately!"

"Yes! And that's behind us, now."

"You're insane."

"We've known each other nearly a year. I understand what makes you tick. I've invested more than a quarter million dollars turning you into the person you are today. And regardless of what happens, I'm going to continue employing and supporting you, if you let me. And have I mentioned I *adore* you? I do. And I love you, too, as you know full well.

And the best part of all?"

"Yeah?"

"You've told me how things are going to be between us, and how they'll be in the future. And I'm okay with it! I'll be the guy who loves you, takes care of you, talks to you day and night, for any reason, anytime you wish. I'll be the guy who makes it possible for you to give yourself to the man of your dreams. And the minute you're ready to do so, I'll step aside."

Maybe shakes her head.

"What?" Sam says.

"I don't believe any part of it."

"You know what?"

"What?"

"That's okay too. But let me ask you this: what have you got to lose?"

"Apart from my dignity and self-respect?"

"Yes."

She thinks about it a minute. Then surprises him by saying, "Out of curiosity, let's see what you look like without your clothes."

44.

MOMENTS LATER, SAM gasps, falls off her, rolls onto his back.

"That's it?" Maybe says.

"For now. Sorry."

"Thirty seconds?"

"What can I say? I was excited."

"Jesus. I thought, you know, an older guy?"

"What about it?"

"I thought that was the big thing about older guys. They're able to hold out longer."

"Look. You need practice, I need practice."

Maybe gives a half smile. "That's sort of sweet."

"Thanks. Anyway, being sexually satisfied is not what's important right now."

"That's easy for *you* to say."

"You know what I mean. The big news is we achieved having sex. Without pain."

"True. The problem is I didn't feel anything at all."

"You must've felt *something*."

"I don't mean to hurt your feelings."

Sam frowns. "Give me a minute."

"Why, you want to fuck me two more times?"

"Funny. Can I ask you something?"

"What?"

"Why won't you let me take off your top?"

"I'm a mess up there."

"That can't be true."

"I'm self-conscious about my breasts."

"Why?"

"I don't want to talk about it."

"But that's the point. You don't have to worry what you say to me."

"They go in different directions."

"Let me have a look."

"You're a pervert."

"Let me see."

She shows him. "See what I mean?"

"These are great boobs. But yeah, I see what you mean."

"I can't show these to someone I love."

"Someone who loves you won't care."

"I'll care."

"Then I'll get them fixed."

"How?"

"This is the simplest surgery in the world. Thirty minutes, tops. Two weeks recovery."

"What're you, a plastic surgeon?"

"No. But a few stitches on the inside here," he points, "and here…and you're perfect."

"Are you sure?"

"Positive."

"Will the stitches show?"

"No. They'll be hidden under here…and here."

"Will it hurt?"

"A little. But it'll be worth it. To you."

"Thanks, Sam."

"My pleasure. And speaking of pleasure, I believe I'm

ready, if you're willing."

She frowns. "I suppose you've earned another shot."

He flips her over.

"What do you think you're doing?" she says.

"Practicing. Let me know if I hurt you in any way."

"Don't worry, you'll know."

He enters her, and the experience makes him light-headed. He pulls her back, so that she's on her knees, and after a couple of minutes, he hears her moaning softly. He's behind her, and she can't see the smile on his face. Nor could she possibly know what he's thinking at this very moment, which is, *I'm fucking Donovan Creed's daughter!*

When they're done, he says, "Will you keep killing for me?"

"Yes," she says. "If you keep paying me."

"We make a perfect team."

"What on earth makes you think that?

"You're willing to kill for me, and I'm willing to die for you."

45.

"HOW MUCH ARE you paying the other girl?" Maybe says.

"What girl?" Sam says.

"The one who's been taking my classes at Mabry."

"Twenty grand."

"For twenty grand the best she can do is a B-plus in biology?"

"Like I said, the professor's a dick."

Maybe laughs. "That's what I told my father."

"You spoke to him?"

"Of course."

"I thought you weren't taking his calls."

"If I ignore my father too long, he starts checking around."

"You wouldn't tell him about any of this, would you?"

"Are you crazy? He'd kill you."

"Yes."

Maybe studies his face a minute. "Aren't you afraid I'll tell him?"

"Should I be?"

"Yes. If you ever displease me enough, you're toast."

"Then promise you'll never tell."

"I won't promise that."

"Will you at least promise not to mention my name?"

"We'll see. Right now he thinks you're a post-Rapture pet salesman named Chuck."

"You're shitting me!"

Maybe laughs.

After ordering room service, Sam drives her home. Tries to kiss her at the door, but she puts her hand between their faces to block his lips.

"We don't have that type of relationship," she says. "Remember?"

"Sorry. I'll check around, find the best doctor for the boob job. I'll let you know when and where."

"We'll have a meeting first, right?"

"You and the doctor? Of course."

"Thanks again for that."

"My pleasure."

Kimberly enters her apartment, locks the door behind her, heads for the kitchen, sees the message light blinking. She presses the button, hears her father's voice. She looks at the digital clock on the oven. Eight fifty-five a.m. Which makes it five fifty-five in Vegas.

She calls her father, gets his voice mail. Leaves a message. "You said to call anytime before nine. I stupidly assumed you'd wait till the last minute to hear from me. But no. It's exactly eight fifty-five, and you're nowhere to be found. Thanks a *lot*!"

46.

"HELLO?" SAM SAYS.

"Was it everything you hoped it would be?" Doc Howard says.

"What are you talking about?"

They're on the phone, Sam driving to the airport, Doc Howard, somewhere in Virginia.

"Do I really have to say it out loud?" Doc Howard says. "It's vulgar."

"I honestly don't know what you're talking about."

"I'm talking about you and Kimberly Creed."

"What about us?"

"You're forcing me to say it? Fine. You fucked her. Was it all you hoped it would be?"

"How did you know?"

"It's my job to know."

"Did you have someone following me?"

"Following *and* listening."

"*How?* We were in a *hotel* room, for crissakes!"

"Doesn't matter. It's time to start paying the piper. Get off at exit 24-B, turn right, drive a half-mile to the bowling alley. Park there, and I'll call you back."

"How will you know when I park?"

"I've got a tracking device on your car."

"I'm trying to catch a plane."

"I know all about the flight. You'll have plenty of time to catch it."

Sam clicks his phone off and sighs. From where he is, the drive to exit 24-B will take ten minutes, a sufficient amount of time to reflect on how he and Doc Howard became allies in Sam's war against Donovan Creed.

47.

Six Weeks Earlier...

SIX WEEKS AGO, Doc Howard treated Sam for a nasty snakebite. Toward the end of the treatment, the two men sat down and had an interesting talk, during which Doc Howard said, "Apart from providing the snake that bit you, why do you hate Donovan Creed so much?"

Sam said, "He destroyed my life."

"How so?"

"Why should I tell *you*? You *work* for the bastard!"

Doc Howard smiled. "You might be surprised how my path and yours can intersect to your benefit. Tell me more."

"Creed stole my wife, put me out of business, and cheated my investors out of billions of dollars."

"What type of investors?"

"I was hiding money for the world's most dangerous people. Creed kidnapped my wife, Rachel, threatened to kill her if I didn't give him the access codes to the funds. He wound up stealing every last cent, then he and Rachel revealed they'd been having an affair for six months. She's been with him ever since."

"They walked away and left you with nothing?"

"He cut me a check for a percentage of the take. As if that would compensate me for stealing Rachel and putting my life in jeopardy."

"He's your arch enemy," Doc Howard said.

"Like Superman and Lex Luthor."

"And you see yourself as the good guy."

"Aren't I?"

"Well, *I* think so, but what do I know? I'm an old man."

"What *do* you know?" Sam said.

"I know Rachel carries the gene that can cure the Spanish Flu. I also know she's been taken to Area B, at Mount Weather."

"Wait," Sam said. "*You* know where Rachel is, but Creed *doesn't*? How's that possible?"

"It's my job to know things."

"Your job as a doctor?"

"I'm many things, including a physician. But let's talk about you."

"What about me?"

"From what I understand, you're a computer genius."

"So?"

"If you could find a way to get into Mount Weather, and work there, we could form an alliance that would benefit both of us."

Sam said, "If you know about Rachel, you probably already know I've been selected to live and work in Area B. With Rachel."

Doc Howard smiled.

Sam said, "If you have access to this type of information, how could I possibly help you?"

"I don't have physical access to the facility."

"Why not?"

"The President trusts me to perform surgery on him, but not to be near the pretty things hidden away in Area B."

"You want me to steal government secrets for you?"

"I'm not sure *what* I want just yet. But I won't ask anything of you that you can't deliver."

"And what would I get out of it?"

"Two things: first, I can deliver the sweetest revenge against Creed you could possibly imagine. Second, I can allow you to stay alive."

"Tell me about the revenge part," Sam said.

"You might find this hard to believe, but I've been communicating with Donovan Creed's twenty-year-old daughter, Kimberly, for nearly a year. Ever since he stopped having her followed."

"So?"

"You're a computer expert, Sam. I'm a mind control expert."

"Go on."

"I "met" her on a social media site and quickly talked her into giving me her phone number. I began calling her, probing her, learning her secrets."

"Why would she talk to you? You're old enough to be her grandfather."

"She doesn't know how old I am, but believes I'm old enough to be her father. I used a voice altering device. You probably think something like that would scare the average young lady, but as you may get the opportunity to learn, Kimberly is not your average young lady."

"What do you mean?"

"She's inherited the killing gene from her father."

"That's possible?"

"Entirely. And I've hired someone to pose as Kimberly at her college, taking her classes, so she could be trained by professional assassins. At first she didn't know they were assassins. She thought they were kickboxing champions and exercise experts who were getting her in shape. But after getting her in shape, they taught her how to fight, how to shoot, and lately they've taught her about poisons."

"To what end?"

"To turn her into a paid assassin."

Sam listened to all this with his mouth hanging open. "Does Creed know?"

"Of course not."

"This is insane."

"Why?"

"How can someone who's never met the girl get her to start killing people based on a telephone relationship?"

"She actually killed a boy before I contacted her. So she had the raw talent and innate ability to begin with. The rest is mind control. And, of course, I believe she inherited the most important quality a contract killer can have."

"What's that?"

"A taste for killing."

"You mean she likes it?"

"She's a natural. Of course, there's a very thin line between being a contract killer and a serial killer. If she's not guided properly, Kimberly could easily go off the deep end."

Sam was speechless.

"So anyway," Doc Howard said, "I found her deepest, darkest secret, and moved forward from there."

"What's her secret?"

"I'll tell you, if we work a deal."

"I'm in."

"You haven't heard the deal."

"Okay, tell me."

"What you get is Kimberly. You won't have complete control over her mind and body, but you'll be well-positioned to influence her."

"Influence her to do what?

"Steal for you, kill for you, and possibly even sleep with you, if that's your wish."

"Turn Creed's daughter into a killer and get her to fall in love with me? This is a joke, right? I bet Creed's watching us right now on a monitor somewhere!"

Sam looked around the room.

"If you recall, the monitors in this room have been destroyed or removed. You'll have your proof within minutes, if I get what I want. But let me address the idea of getting her to fall in love with you. I wouldn't count on that happening. But you're a hop, skip and a jump from being able to seduce her."

"You said you can furnish proof?"

"I've made tapes of every conversation I've had with Kimberly. Hundreds of hours. I'll turn those over to you, to study carefully over the next few weeks. I'll sneak you onto some of our calls so you can get a real-time feel for the way I work her mind. When you're ready, you can take over. In your real voice."

"Won't she know it's not you?"

"No. You'll have memorized our entire history of conversations. You'll have me down cold." He pauses. "But there is one issue you'll have to get past."

"What's that?"

"I've made her call me Daddy."

"What? Why?"

"Part of the mind control. She craves her father's love, so I'm transferring that emotion. She's a very smart young lady. She knows I'm manipulating her. Which gives her the false sense she's maintaining control in the relationship. But her

180

weakness is logic. If you can make an extremely logical case for something, you can probably get her to do it."

"I could make it sound logical to fall in love with me."

"She's twenty."

"So?"

"Girls that age are biologically drawn to strong young men of a similar age. Love is not a logical act."

"What do you mean?"

"I'm not saying it's impossible to make her fall in love with you, but I doubt you can. Your age and your looks are acceptable, but not an advantage for a nice looking twenty-year-old, in my opinion. Killing and copulating are acts. They're specific, physical acts that take place and are quickly ended. Love is an emotion. It's a feeling you have, not an act you perform."

"Example?"

"Do you ever play poker?"

"I've played a couple of times."

"And Kimberly's fallen in love a couple of times."

"So?"

"Trying to get you to play poker with me at one o'clock this afternoon is an act. I might have to persist, but I could probably talk you into playing a few games of poker with me today, or some other day. But trying to talk you into become a professional poker player today is too much to shoot for. Do you understand?"

"Getting her to fuck me is easier than getting her to fall in love with me."

"Crude, but accurate."

"And she calls you Daddy."

"She calls me Daddy, yes. And she goes by the name, Maybe Taylor. Thinks I don't know Taylor's the name of the young man she killed. Her former boyfriend. In fact, I'm not supposed to know anything about the boyfriend, so put that part out of your mind."

"Why Maybe?"

"Her choice of names. It means maybe she'll kill for me, maybe she won't. It's her way of not having to think about killing as a profession."

"The Daddy thing will be hard to navigate around, if I'm going to seduce her."

"You'll work it out. She already loves me, or at least, the *idea* of me. I'm her closest confidante, her only true friend. But I haven't taken our relationship into any sort of sexual area. It's a logical extension for her, but impractical for me. You, on the other hand, are young enough. And you're cunning, and manipulating, given you haven't tipped your hand to Creed about Area B. And Kimberly's extremely vulnerable to a sexual relationship."

"Why's that?"

"She has female problems that can be exploited. She thinks I'm older, despite the voice disguising equipment. So when you speak to her in your real voice, she'll be curious enough to open her mind to the possibility of romance. At that point you can confess you've fallen for her."

"You think it'll work?"

"Yes."

"Because?"

"She's dying to feel loved. It's your ticket to ride."

"That's a pretty hip comment."

"I have my moments."

Sam took a minute to work it around in his mind. Then said, "I understand the Daddy thing. But it places a huge obstacle in my path."

"You need to let that go. It's not as big an issue as you think. It helped convince her the best way to earn her father's respect and love is to excel at what he does."

"What, kill people?"

"Yes."

"She's seeking his approval."

"Exactly."

"And *will* he approve?"

"I can't answer that or *any* question about how Creed might react to a given situation. And I say this after studying him for twenty years."

"He's a true psychopath, isn't he?"

"No. His assistant, Callie Carpenter's a true psychopath."

"I know about that from personal experience. She nearly killed me once."

"If she wanted to kill you, you'd be dead."

"Creed stepped in."

"He saved your life?"

"Yeah. Twice, in fact. But it doesn't count."

"Why not?"

"He only saved my life after kidnapping and mentally torturing me."

"So you still want revenge."

"I'd give ten years of my life to make him suffer a day. Until you happened along, my best shot was forcing him to know Rachel and I were underground together, beyond his reach. But I have a sinking feeling he might be pleased when he finds she's stuck in a bunker for a few months or years."

"You may be right about that."

"But she's supposed to be his girlfriend."

"Yes, but Creed's in a category unto himself."

"And Kimberly?"

"She's a different breed altogether. A cold-blooded killer, but completely predictable. At least, for now."

"How would this work?"

"I can arrange murder-for-hire contracts that will come directly to you, and you can farm them out through Kimberly, and another lady who works for me, Hailey Brimstone."

"Brimstone? Are you for real?"

"You've met her."

"I don't think so."

Doc Howard pressed a button on his cell phone. "Lou? I'm with Sam. Can you bring Hailey in here?"

When the guy named Lou showed up with Hailey, Sam did a double-take, because Hailey Brimstone looked exactly like Sam's wife, Rachel.

"I didn't dream it," Sam said. "She was here, in my room when I was half-conscious."

"That's right," Doc Howard said. Then he introduced them and told Hailey he was retiring, but said Sam would continue to provide her with work, if she was interested.

She was.

Sam watched every movement Hailey made while she was in the room. When she left, he said, "Creed recruited her to mess with my head?"

"Yes."

"I am definitely in. Tell me about the contracts."

"They'll pay twice what you need to compensate Hailey and Kimberly for their work. You can use the balance to fund your courtship with Kimberly."

"Do we plan to tell Creed what we've done to his daughter?"

"That's up to you. But the longer it continues, the sweeter the revenge. You're manipulating her into the family business, so to speak. Though Creed is unpredictable, it's likely he'll be devastated to learn his daughter has turned into a murderer. If you *really* want to punish him you could possibly get her to commit terrorist acts. And imagine how he'll feel when he learns Sam Case is coupling his daughter!"

"Coupling?"

"I'm old. Screwing her."

"We say fuck."

"Of course you do. Screwing isn't vulgar enough. Very well, you'll be fucking Donovan Creed's daughter, and she'll be killing for you. Could there possibly be a better revenge?"

"Killing Callie Carpenter would sweeten the pot."

"You've got enough on your plate with this."

"You haven't said what you want from me."

"You'll earn your keep."

"What will I have to do?"

"More than two things, less than six."

"Are they legal?"

"What do you think?"

"Doesn't matter. I'm in."

"I thought you might be."

"Can I ask you why you did this to Kimberly? I thought you were Creed's friend."

"In the business we share, the concept of right and wrong is blurry, and lines are often crossed. It's wise to give Donovan Creed a reason not to kill you. I recently had power over him, then I lost it. I always like to have something in reserve. His daughter is one of his weaknesses."

"He's got others?"

"Yes."

"Such as?"

"Your wife, Rachel."

"What's Kimberly's deepest, darkest secret?"

"She suffers from vaginismus."

"What's that?"

Doc Howard spent the next thirty minutes explaining vaginismus, and the effect it's had on Kimberly.

Sam ended the conversation saying, "It's a slam dunk!"

Doc Howard said, "What is?"

"Using Kimberly to punish Creed."

48.

Present Day, Present Time...

SAM PULLS INTO the parking lot of the bowling alley, and waits.

Within seconds, Doc Howard calls and says, "To start things off, I want the Bin Laden death photos."

"*What*?"

"You heard me."

"How the hell—?"

"Sam? The government keeps the most valuable documents, photographs, paintings, patents, and other treasures underground, in Area B. You live and work there."

"Those things are locked up in a whole different part of the complex. There's never been a security breach in the history of the facility!"

"You're a computer expert, with full access to the government's computers."

"No one gets full access."

"Good thing you're a computer expert."

"You expect me to hack into the government's computers? The most sophisticated system in the *world*?"

"Don't be so dramatic. I know twelve-year-old kids who could do it. You just happen to be the guy on the inside."

"You want the actual photographs or the digital images?"

"One should be as good as the other."

"If we're talking about the digital prints, I can probably deliver them, if they're in the computer."

"You know damn well they are. They digitally catalog every item in the vaults."

"What are your plans for the photos?"

"That's my business."

"What if I refuse?"

"You'll be dead before we end the call."

"How?"

"Remember the tracking device in your rental car? We planted explosives under the driver's seat. But don't try to run, or I'll have to do this."

"What?"

Sam hears a click.

"Did you just lock my doors?"

"I did. You're spam in a can."

"I don't understand the reference."

"It sucks being old. Though you might never know."

"Look," Sam says. "Not saying I'd ever double cross you, but what if I said sure, I'll help you, but change my mind later, when I get back in the bunker?"

"You may be able to survive in there for many months. But sooner or later the government will release you. When they do, I'll catch you, and turn you over to Creed."

"And if Creed's dead?"

"Callie. Are you, in fact, refusing to get me the photos?"

"No, of course not."

"Good. So answer the question I asked earlier."

"Which one?"

"Was having sex with Kimberly everything you hoped it would be?"

188

"Yes. And then some."

"Good. I love it when a plan comes together. How did it make you *feel*?"

"Great. You knew it would, and it did. It felt, and *still* feels great."

"You're not falling in love with her, are you?"

"No chance. Kimberly Creed is inferior to me in every possible way. And now I've made her my fuck pony."

"Was it hard to bed her?"

Sam laughs. "Fucking her was child's play! And I'll continue to fuck her as long as it suits me, though she's not much of a lay. If not for the connection to Creed, I wouldn't travel across town to do her."

"One last question, if I'm not being too nosey. While you were having sex with Kimberly Creed, who were you thinking about, Donovan? Or Kimberly?"

"Both."

"Good for you, Sam."

49.

Doc Howard

DOC HOWARD PRESSES the rewind button for the third time. *"Was having sex with Kimberly everything you hoped it would be?"*

"Yes. And then some."

He fast forwards to *"Kimberly Creed is inferior to me in every possible way. And now I've made her my fuck pony."*

He fast forwards to *"Fucking her was child's play! And I'll continue to fuck her as long as it suits me, though she's not much of a lay. If not for the connection to Creed, I wouldn't travel across town to do her."*

Doc Howard smiles, thinking of the many ways he can use it. The big question is who should he play it for first? Sam, Donovan, or Kimberly?

He tries to give an evil villain laugh, but starts coughing in the middle of it.

Getting old's a bitch.

50.

Maybe Taylor

KIMBERLY LIKES HAVING an alias. For one thing, it helps her separate her killing life from her personal life. She also likes Sam far more than she thought she would. He grows on you. *Like a wart*, she thinks, smiling.

What she doesn't like is her current relationship with her father. Specifically, she doesn't like the way *she's* been treating *him*. He's got a life, and she's a grown woman. They live in separate states, and his job keeps him traveling from place to place on a moment's notice. She's only recently begun to understand that part, but she now understands why it's hard to schedule visits in advance.

And her father has enemies.

And those enemies might decide to come after her, to get back at him. He has to worry he could be leading those sorts of people to his daughter every time he meets her someplace.

Of course, this is one of the main reasons she decided to work for Sam almost a year ago. When he talked about helping her get in shape and learn self-defense, she thought of her father. If she could protect herself, maybe he wouldn't worry so much about her safety. Then, over months, as she and Sam became closer, she told him about her father, what he did for a living, and Sam said he could provide her with that type of teaching as well. She didn't have to kill people if she didn't want to. But wouldn't it be nice to know how?

From there, it was just a hop, skip and a jump—as Sam would say—to wondering how it felt to kill someone. Not a spur-of-the-moment killing, like with her boyfriend, Taylor, but a premeditated one, like her father routinely performs.

What better way could there be to understand his psyche than to enter his world?

After the breakthrough with Sam today, her head's in a good place. Her female plumbing seems to have been restored, and she's on the threshold of what could be a budding romance with an older guy who happens to be her adoring boss. For all the protesting she's done, she's secretly excited about having Sam as her boyfriend.

With so many things going for her, she suddenly regrets the phone message she left for her father.

She calls him back, gets his voice mail again. Says, "I'm sorry about the message I left a few minutes ago. I didn't mean to say those things. I'm booking a flight to Vegas as soon as I hang up. I'm coming today, because we need to talk. There've been some major changes in my life, and I want to discuss them with you. I can't say you'll be happy with them, but I'm in a happy place. You've always said if I'm happy, you're happy. So we'll see. Anyway, call my cell if there's a problem. Otherwise, I'm on my way to Vegas to see if we can be friends again."

51.

Donovan Creed

JEFF AND I sleep most of the way to Chicago. About an hour out, I give Bob Koltech a sack of cash and have him order a limo on his dime, so I won't leave a paper trail.

"How much extra to spend the night here?" I ask.

"Just our rooms, food and transportation," Bob says.

"How's five grand sound?"

"Generous."

I peel off fifty bills from one of the stacks in my case and add it to Bob's bag.

"Don't buy any liquor with that," I say.

"What time you want to leave tomorrow?" he asks.

"I don't know. We might even leave this afternoon, if my lady friend wants to come to Vegas."

"Okay then. No liquor."

When we land, Bennie the limo driver's waiting for us with a stretch limo and a big smile. "You guys headed to UIC?" he says.

"We are," I say.

"Good thing I'm your driver," he says.

"Why's that?"

"UIC has more than a hundred buildings on campus."

"Over how many acres?"

"Two hundred forty."

Bennie's a proud father. Because his son is enrolled at UIC's medical school, we get the full lecture on the ride over. The part I remember, UIC's the nation's largest medical school and has an annual budget of more than three hundred million dollars. Bennie claims thirty-five percent of the students speak English as a second language, which impresses him, for some reason.

"That's amazing!" I say, noting the smirk on Jeff's face.

Bennie says, "Which building you want?"

"Center for Magnetic Resonance Research."

"Never heard of it."

I punch the information into my cell phone. "1801 West Taylor Street."

"Oh. You shoulda said MRI. So, you gonna enter the beast?"

"We're just doing a short tour."

"If you've got a pacemaker, or any metal inside you, they won't let you near the beast. Can't even enter the building! That's the big boy I'm talkin' about, the biggest MRI machine in the world."

"Maybe we'll get to see it," I say.

Bennie looks up in the mirror to catch my eye. He nods his head to the side, indicating Jeff. "He don't talk much, does he?"

"English is his third language."

"No shit?"

"Hakuna uchafu," Jeff says.

Bennie says, "What's that?"

"Swahili," Jeff says.

"No shit?"

Jeff smiles. "Exactly."

Jeff and I enter the building. The small leather bag slung over my shoulder contains toiletries, a change of clothes, and a gun. The suitcase in my hand contains what's left of the cash after paying Bob for the flight and his overnight expenses.

I look around till I spot what I'm looking for, an old man and his wife. Jeff heads to the reception area to strike up a conversation with the two ladies working the desk.

As I approach the elderly couple I say, "Which of you is getting scanned this morning?"

The woman has a patch over one eye, and her other one is rheumy and filled with cataracts. Nevertheless, she thinks she knows me.

"I'd know you anywhere!" she squeals.

"You would?"

"You're that movie star, what's-his-name!"

"No."

"You *are*! I'd know you *anywhere*!"

I wink at her and say, "Please, I'm trying to stay in character."

She giggles, displaying the whitest set of dentures I've ever seen. It makes no sense anything on the planet earth could be this white! Herman Melville spent the entire Chapter 42 of *Moby-Dick* trying to explain how white the whale was, but Moby had nothing on this lady.

White teeth aside, she's right. I *do* strongly resemble the famous movie star whose name currently escapes her, except that I've gone back to my original black hair color. When Doc Howard, Dr. Petrovsky, and their team of surgeons reconstructed my face, attempting to give me a new identity, they used a movie star's photo as a guide. Personally, I liked my old face better, though I did have an enormous scar on it back then.

"I love your eyes!" she says.

Of course she does. They're back to the original jade green color I was born with, now that I've stopped wearing those ridiculous blue contact lenses.

"I'm Mildred," she says. "But you can call me Millie. And this is Walt. He's the one with the nine o'clock appointment."

Walt appears to be near death, but raises his eyebrows as if to say hi. I don't speak eyebrow, so I just say "Hi Walt."

Millie winks at me with her one eye. Or maybe she blinked. It's hard to tell. She says, "If I were twenty years younger…" then her voice trails off.

If she were twenty years younger she'd what? I wonder. Twenty years younger would *still* make her fifty years older than Miranda!

I sit beside her, despite the fact I think she's coming on to me. She pats my arm. I wonder if there's an eye underneath the patch, then decide I don't want to know.

"I can't believe it's *you*!" Millie says.

I get that a lot. You'd think people would come up with something more intelligent, but inevitably they say, *I can't believe it's you*.

Who else would I be? Who else would *anyone* be?

But wait. Millie's not finished.

"Is it really *you*?" she says. "Are you really sitting right here next to me?"

She's making as much sense as Ricky Ricardo singing 'You Picked a Fine Time to Leave Me, Lucille.'

Then again, I recently asked a woman if she was okay after watching her walk into a lamp post and fall on her ass.

Before her head blew up.

"What's in the suitcase?" Millie asks.

"Money."

196

"Aw, you shouldn't have!" she says, jokingly.

"Let me ask you a question."

"Shoot!"

"Are you and Walt rich?"

Millie starts cackling.

Even Walt's eyebrows manage to smile.

"I've got a proposition for you," I say.

"Didja hear that, Walt? He's propositioning me!"

This time I don't try to interpret Walt's eyebrows. I say, "Millie, I've got a five-forty appointment to be scanned today. If you're willing to swap appointments with me, I'll give you twenty thousand dollars cash."

Millie gasps.

I look her in the eye. "What do you say?"

"Twenty thousand dollars…and a kiss!" She says.

Oh no, *oh hell no*! I'm thinking. But what I say is, "How lucky for me!"

Millie doesn't just kiss me, she tongues the shit out of me! And hers is not an ordinary tongue, either. It's a flippin' freak of nature! It's long, thick, and dry, and feels like sawdust wadding up in the back of my throat. I have to fight to hold back the gag reflex. As she extricates her tongue, her dentures dislodge. I feel like I'm going to be sick, but moments later, she speaks to the receptionist with me standing there, and before you know it, I've got Walt's appointment.

I ask Jeff to check the inner offices, where I'll have to change into one of those silly hospital gowns, even though they're only scanning my brain. While he's in there, I tell Norma the receptionist that if my scan turns out to be normal, I'm going to ask my girlfriend to marry me. I hand her the small gift-wrapped box.

"I haven't told anyone about this, not even Jeff," I say.

"Why not?" Norma says.

"I want it to be a surprise. Will you hold it for me, just until I come out?"

"Well, I'm not really supposed to hold items for patients."

"Please? It would mean the world to me!"

"We have lockers."

She tries to hand it back to me.

"Please? I'm not comfortable leaving it in a locker. It'll only be twenty minutes."

She sighs. "Okay."

"Can you put it in your pocket?"

She sighs again. "Fine."

"Promise not to tell anyone?"

"I promise," she says, rolling her eyes.

"I hope my scan is normal," I say.

Norma looks doubtful, but says, "I hope so, too."

I get the impression she feels bad for my girlfriend.

52.

BEFORE HEADING INTO one of the dressing rooms to change into my hospital gown, I check my messages and notice Kimberly called.

I press the play button, and frown as I hear her angry words. She waited until five minutes before the deadline to call and has the gall to be mad at me for not being available.

Great.

I see she left me a second message, minutes later. Probably worked herself into a rage after thinking about it a while longer. Her mother used to do that. I stare at the screen a minute and decide to ignore the second message. I just don't have the strength for her sullen attitude right now. She can chew me out later.

Jeff says, "You want me to hold anything for you?"

"No, but I'd like you to guard my locker while I'm in there."

"Will do."

"Are you okay spending the night?" I say. "If not, I can get you a flight back to Vegas."

"I'm good. I'll find something to do."

"Okay, then."

The technician joins us for a short chat. I tell him not to freak when he sees the chip in my brain. "Let me know if it's operable," I say.

"We just shoot the pictures," he says. "We don't interpret them."

I nod, then follow him into the scanning room, and take my position on the table.

"Just do twenty minutes worth," I say.

"It doesn't work that way. You'll be here the full forty minutes," he says.

Great.

53.

"YOU WEREN'T LYING," the technician says. "I've never seen anything like that before."

"Do I get some sort of prize?"

"If you do, it won't come from us."

"Story of my life," I say.

I exit the room and find Jeff standing with his back to my locker.

"Any problems?" I say.

"Were you expecting any?"

"I wasn't sure what to expect."

"They had you in there forty minutes," he says. "Is your brain that much larger than you thought?"

"Yeah."

"Did it hurt?"

"Nope."

I think about pressing the button now, to see if the MRI worked, but then a scary thought crosses my mind. Specifically, I wonder how much damage I might do. Assuming the chip in my head has been erased, I'm safe. But when I press the button on the ceramic device four times, two hundred and twelve chips are going to explode, wherever they are in the world!

Some of the chips are bound to be attached to explosives.

Plastic explosives—plastique as we call it—is soft and easily molded by hand. How easy? Explosives engineers call them "putty explosives." So a group of terrorists on the same plane can each walk into an airplane lavatory carrying small bits of plastique and add their bit to the others that have been placed underneath and behind areas that aren't easily visible. Like under the sink. Push a chip into the plastique, and you're looking at a bomb that can be detonated from virtually anywhere in the world.

Even this locker room at the MRI center.

Here's how my brain works: what if the airplane lavatory scenario is in place on Miranda's flight? When I press the button, maybe the plane explodes, and I wind up killing 300 innocent people, including Miranda, simply because I'd been hoping to kill a couple dozen terrorists. Would I be able to live with myself?

I doubt it.

So there's that. On the other hand, the longer I wait before pressing the button, the more time the terrorists will have to set bombs in and around high profile targets!

Want to see how the dark side of my brain works?

What if I'm being set up?

What if George was a terrorist, and the whole lady-walking-into-a-lamp post event was staged for my benefit? A good mastermind could have put that into play. Now that I think about it, George was awfully quick to tell me there was no need to meet his arms dealer. What if there *was* no arms dealer? What if his terrorist buddies have truckloads of plastique stashed all over downtown Las Vegas? Or maybe the airport? What if the plan was for me to press the button four times and cause the destruction of tens of thousands of innocent people?

I'd love to be the one to press the button. I just wish I could believe the only ones who'll get hurt are the bad guys.

Unfortunately, in real life it doesn't always work that way.

I get dressed and sit on the bench in the locker room, check my phone messages, see that Miranda has texted me her flight information. She'll be here in two hours and forty-five minutes, which means she hasn't left New York City yet.

I look at Jeff. "You want some breakfast?"

"If it's real breakfast," he says.

"What's real to you?"

"Rooster knees and grits."

"A diner?"

"That'll do."

"Bennie ought to know a place."

Jeff calls Bennie to tell him we're ready to be picked up.

"No problem," Bennie says. "I'm just around the corner."

I retrieve the gift-wrapped present from Norma, the receptionist, and shake it to make sure the device is still inside. Everything feels right. Is that a good or bad sign?

See how I live?

Back in the locker room I open the gift box. The device is there.

Why am I so paranoid?

Because it's all going too easily.

My guard is up.

Jeff and I head outside. My eyes are scanning the campus, expecting an ambush. I watch the car drive up, wonder if it's filled with armed agents bent on retrieving the chip. Or killing me. Or both.

IUC's more of an urban campus, which means there are few trees to hide behind. The gun is no longer in my bag, it's in my pocket, in my hand. I feel like an old-time gunslinger, ready to start shootin' the minute some owlhoot draws a bead on me.

Then I feel like an idiot when it turns out the car is perfectly safe.

Jeff appears to be looking at me strangely.

I wonder if my present state of mind has something to do with the chip being de-magnetized. Maybe that did something to enhance my paranoia.

I climb in the limo. Jeff scoots near the front to explain to Bennie what type of diner he's looking for. While he's doing that, I call Lou.

"What's up?" Lou says, cheerfully.

"I need to cancel the flight."

"Are you sure?"

"Yeah. I changed my mind."

"What about the chip?"

And there it was.

I say, "I don't recall telling you anything about a chip."

"No?"

"No."

"You must have."

"I don't think so."

"Then how would I know?"

"How indeed?" I say. I must've sounded strange because Jeff turns to look at me.

"You okay?" he says.

I study Jeff a moment. I've known him for six years. I generally trust him, but he's an odd duck, and I don't trust anyone completely. Maybe it's because I was lying on the table, vulnerable, for forty minutes, and haven't recovered from that loss of control yet.

Lou hasn't come up with a response, so I click the phone off and concentrate on Jeff. From where he's sitting, I can't disable him without a full-scale encounter. In other words, he's too far away for me to strike him before he can react. By the same token, I'm too far away for *him* to attack *me*.

Not that he seems the least inclined to do so. Instead, he's trying to touch his nose with the tip of his tongue.

I'm pretty sure Jeff's safe. He sees me staring at him and says, "What?"

"Are you still dating that girl, the one with the weird job?"

He laughs. "The hair boiler?"

"Right. Tell me again what she does?"

"She dumps tons of animal hair into giant vats of boiling water until it curls. She dumps the hair in the pot, stirs it, drains it, dries it."

"I remember she was very pretty," I say.

"Still is."

"There was some reason she had trouble getting dates."

"The smell."

"Tell me again."

"Picture the smell of wet, burning, animal hair. She boils it all day long."

"Boiled hair soup!"

"Exactly. The smell is always in her hair. It even seeps into her skin."

"Would you ever let her cook for you?"

"Yeah, but not soup."

"And you're able to overlook the smell?"

"That's why we get along so well. I like the smell! Why do you ask?"

"I have no idea."

"Just making conversation?"

"I guess."

I spot Kimberly's voice message on my phone. This time I listen to it. Just as I'm done, I get a text from her. She's in

Dallas, waiting on her connecting flight. But it's on time.

"Jeff, we need to cancel breakfast."

"What's wrong?"

"My daughter's on her way to Vegas."

"Right now?"

"Right now."

"What about Miranda?"

"I can't wait that long."

He grins. "Want me to meet her at the airport for you? Make sure she's okay?"

"Not on your life!"

I press the speed dial for Miranda. She answers, saying, "Donovan, I'm so sorry! Our plane's been delayed. But I'll be there before one o'clock."

"Honey, that's actually good news."

"I don't understand. You don't want to see me?"

"Of course I do! But I just found out my daughter's on her way to Vegas to pay me a surprise visit."

She laughs. "That would've been awkward."

"I'll make it up to you."

"Damn right you will," she says.

"I look forward to it."

"Me too."

54.

BOB KOLTECH GETS us back to the private airfield. I pay him the balance I owe him, and he tries to hug me. I back away. He tries to shake hands. I bump his fist, instead. I like Bob, but I don't allow anyone get a hold of me if I can help it.

"How'm I gonna show my love?" he says, frowning.

"By being available for me, day and night."

He grins. "Count on it."

Jeff and I climb in my car and I head straight for McCarran International, knowing Kimberly will be landing any minute. I find a spot in short-term parking and tell Jeff to catch a cab to PhySpa to check on George's corpse.

"If it's ready, what should I do?"

"Start without me."

He smiles. "Thanks, boss."

Jeff is at least a little stranger than the rest of us.

Moments later I'm in baggage claim, talking to Lou on my cell phone.

"Why wouldn't you take my calls?" he says.

"I was on a plane."

"I thought you changed your mind about needing a plane."

I ignore the comment. I should probably be more concerned with what's going on with Lou, but I'm so excited about Kimberly's visit, and so happy about her friendship offer, I barely care. Lou's after me? Big deal. Not so long ago my life was in the hands of a cage full of monkeys!

"I notice you called me three times," I say. "What's up?"

"I wanted to come clean."

That surprises me.

"Go ahead," I say.

"Darwin wanted your itinerary."

"And you gave it to him?"

"He's my boss. You keep forgetting. You fired me, remember?"

It's true. I do keep forgetting. But I don't forget why I fired Lou. He tried to kill me. But I forgave him. Not completely, but enough to let him continue working as my facilitator. Since he and I both work for Darwin, it's not a great idea to keep the relationship going. But Lou is irreplaceable, so I can't imagine finding someone else. Whoever I get would have to be a personal secretary type of person, with no government contacts. And he or she would have to understand what I do for a living, and...well, it's a tough gig.

"You weren't going to tell me about Darwin," I say.

"I hoped to prevent it. It's not like he's using the information to kill you or anything."

"Lou?"

"Yeah?"

"Darwin ordered Doc Howard to plant the chip in my brain."

"That's nearly true."

"What do you mean?"

"I know you don't trust me, and I don't blame you. But I'm the most loyal friend you have."

I take the phone away from my ear and look at it. Then put it back to my ear.

"Did you mean to say that?"

"I know," he says. "Like my old friend Donovan Creed used to say, it sounds stupid when you say it out loud like that."

I smile.

"Let me try to explain," Lou says.

"Make it quick."

"Got a hot date?"

"Something even better."

"Okay. Remember Augustus?"

"Of course."

"If somehow he had survived, and the whole issue with the kidnapped girl had been resolved, would he be able to trust you from that point on?"

"Yes. But what happened with us was different."

"I'm trying to make up for it."

"Then give me something to convince me. Because right now it sounds like you're in Darwin's pocket."

"I decided to give you a present."

"A present."

"Right. Something so big you'll know you can trust me with your life."

"What could possibly be that big?"

"I just killed Doc Howard."

"*What*? Why on earth—"

"Doc Howard was Darwin."

As I'm about to faint from shock, I hear a young woman shout "Father!"

It's Kimberly, heading down the escalator, toward baggage claim.

I tell Lou, "Thanks."

"Is that all you've got to say?"

"No, but it's the first thing."

55.

AFTER HUGGING KIMBERLY, we sit and wait for her luggage. She's beaming. I've never seen her look so happy.

"Let me guess," I say. "You found a golden ticket in your Wonka Bar?"

"Even better."

"You're in love again?"

"Even better. I realized I don't need to be in love to be happy."

I feel her forehead. "Are you feeling okay?"

She smiles.

I say, "You're still a female, right?"

"Don't be a shit head!"

She looks beyond me a second.

"Oh, the poor man!" she says.

I follow her gaze and see a man with two enormous bandages, one on each side of his head.

Tony Spumoni. Carrying a briefcase.

He sees me looking at him and immediately spins around and ducks into the men's room.

"Do you know him?" she asks.

"We've met."

"He seems terrified of you."

My mind begins racing. If there really was an arms dealer, and if George didn't come home last night, is it possible the

210

arms dealer might have started threatening other members of Ropic's board? Could they have coerced Tony into helping them? Like planting a bomb at the airport? I don't know. But one thing I do know is sometimes indecision is worse than a wrong decision. I can't take a chance on the terrorists planting explosives all over the world and setting them off at the same time with the wrist device. Even if there's collateral damage, I'm suddenly convinced fewer civilians will die if I detonate the two hundred and twelve devices right now.

I remove the ceramic device from my pocket, take a deep breath, and press the button four times.

My head is fine, I'm happy to report, but the airport men's room explodes.

I don't know if anyone else was in there, but I know most of Tony Spumoni is not. One of his ears, still casted, rolls to a stop a foot from Kimberly's shoe.

She kicks it away, and the look of shock on my face makes her laugh out loud.

People are screaming. Rushing, running around.

Kimberly's smiling at me. *Smiling*!

"You're not upset?" I say.

"Of course not."

"A bomb just went off in an airport!"

"So?"

The noise around us becomes so loud I have to shout to be heard. "What's going on?" I yell.

"I'm not upset because *you're* not," Kimberly shouts. She leans into my ear so the whole world won't hear her words. "I'm also not upset because I saw you detonate the bomb. And because…"

"Yes?"

"I'm OOU."

211

I give her a puzzled look. "What's that mean?"

She points to herself, then to me, and says, "I'm one of us."

"Tell me," I say.

And she does. People are running around us, yelling and screaming, but as far as I can see, there's no damage beyond what happened in the men's room. There's a TV monitor twenty feet away, suspended from the ceiling, and I glance at it from time to time while Kimberly tells her story. I'm trying to see if there's any breaking news of planes falling from the sky or buildings blowing up.

So far, so good.

But it's early.

Kimberly's story is compelling, as is the TV monitor. She's telling me she lied about being in school and how she hasn't attended classes for the past two semesters. I don't know what to think about that, because Lou obtained a copy of her transcripts. Her biology teacher's a dick, remember?

But I don't interrupt her.

The whole scene around us is surreal. Security guards are shouting, trying to make their way into the men's room. People are running here and there, some have left their bags, others are stealing bags off the moving luggage belt. Someone's making crowd control announcements, trying to get us to evacuate the building. Everyone's yelling at everyone else, but no one seems to notice the two of us.

"Keep an eye out for your suitcase," I say.

"I am."

The area around us grows less noisy, and Kimberly no longer has to shout. She tells me she's had a certain type of female problem she really can't discuss, but that a man befriended her almost a year ago, and became her confidante, and gave her confidence, and uplifted her.

"Who is this man?" I say.

"Not important," she says, then tells me how the man helped her understand the cause of her depression. He convinced her that what she really craved above all else in the world was her father's love. When she gets to that point, she bursts into tears and hugs me, and I forget all about the TV monitor.

But when Kimberly calms down and tells me how the man paid for her psychiatric visits and kickboxing and weapons training, and how he taught her the family business of killing people—I felt like I was in the middle of a Fellini movie.

Now we're being rounded up with the others and ordered to go outside. Kimberly sees her suitcase. We grab it and head outside.

"What do you mean you killed people? You mean you killed them in your mind? Metaphorically?"

She laughs. "No, father. I killed them in real life."

I look at her with grave concern. I wonder if she's crazy.

"You haven't actually killed a human being," I say.

"Yes."

"When? How?"

She smiles. "I have your interest *now*, don't I?"

I frown. "You do."

Something suddenly clicks.

"This man," I say.

"What about him?"

"Did he disguise his voice?"

She pauses too long before answering, "How do you mean?"

She's lying. But why?

I say, "What I'm asking, did he use a voice altering device?"

"Not that I know of."

213

"You'd know."

"Then I guess not."

"You're certain?"

"Yes, of course. Why are you asking that?"

We start heading for my car. When we get there, I hold the passenger door open for her, and call Callie while putting Kimberly's suitcase in the trunk. When Callie answers I say, "Are you with me or against me?"

"What are you talking about?"

"I want to know who I can count on. You've made some remarks lately that bothered me. I have trust issues. You know that."

"Of course. And abandonment issues."

"Right."

"And emotional issues, and mental issues, and issues with women, and psychotic episodes, and schizophrenic issues and—"

"Enough! Can I count on you?"

"Of course. Why?"

"I'm declaring war."

"On whom?"

"Darwin."

"Oh, shit!"

"But he might be dead already."

"You're not making sense."

"Me or him, Callie?"

"You, of course."

"Will you help me?"

"I'll pull the fucking trigger. Is that enough help?"

"Thanks."

"Is that all you've got to say?"

"No. But it's the first thing."

56.

IN THE CAR now, still at the airport's short-term parking, waiting for the line of cars to thin out so we can leave. The place is a total traffic jam, and it looks like we're going to be here awhile.

Kimberly has grown silent, trying to gauge my reaction.

"I'm stunned by this revelation," I say, "but I just blew up two hundred and twelve blasting caps all over the world. I need to listen to the radio a minute to make sure the airport bathroom isn't the only thing I damaged."

She nods.

"You're okay with that?" I say.

"Of course, father. We're working together now. I'm going to be on your team."

"You are?"

"You do have a team, right?"

"I do. But this isn't a game."

"Of course not. It's life and death."

I look at her a moment, then turn my attention to the radio news. The reporter is saying they have reports of numerous explosions in the general Las Vegas area, including the airport. Furthermore, at the precise time the airport bomb went off, small explosions were reported all over the country. But so far no one has reported any significant damage. It's all two people were killed here, one there, and so forth.

I'm beginning to think the decision to detonate was not only timely, but sound. In the days to come, I bet the vast majority of deaths will turn out to be members of Darwin's terrorist watch list.

I think about Doc Howard being Darwin all this time. He's never spoken to me without using voice altering equipment, the quality of which has improved dramatically over the years. Though I had no way of knowing who Darwin was, I never would have suspected Doc Howard. I don't know if Darwin was my enemy or not, or if he was planning to ambush me in Chicago, had I kept the original appointment. I don't know why he might have wanted me dead, or even if he did. Nor do I know for certain he's dead. I mean, all I've got to go on is Lou's word. Maybe Lou killed Doc Howard to throw me off the scent. Maybe Lou is Darwin! Or maybe Doc Howard really *is* Darwin, and he and Lou faked his death. If he's alive, he might still want to kill me.

I'll want proof Doc Howard was Darwin, and I'll want proof of his death. If it turns out Darwin's alive, I'll find and kill him, because I don't like the way he's forced me to live. I'm wealthy. I don't need to work for the government. With Darwin out of the picture I can concentrate on living a simpler life. There's a chip in my head that'll require extensive surgery to remove, thanks to him. If Doc was Darwin he *personally* planted the chip in my brain. Worse, he got me to pay him a hundred million dollars to *disable* it!

Genius.

That's what Darwin is.

A genius.

Kimberly can deny it all she wants, but there's no doubt in my mind that Darwin's behind her transformation from school girl to killer, assuming she's actually done what she claims.

216

"How many people have you killed?" I ask.

"Eight or nine, something like that."

"In killing, eight or nine is a big difference."

"You think?"

"For a twenty-year-old girl? Yes."

"Fine. Let me count."

She does. Out loud. When she gets to number three, Professor Jonah Toth, I know she's telling the truth. Because he's the guy who used to follow Kimberly until about a year ago. Lou and I knew him as Jimmy T.

"Where did you kill Toth?"

"Viceroy College, Charleston, South Carolina. Men's room. Shall I keep counting?"

"By all means."

She continues to count. Along the way I ask a few questions. She tells me how she handled the Mayor and his aides, and their hookers, and another woman, and I remember I'd read something about the incident, and how these people had been murdered in a beach house.

Kimberly stops at nine.

"The man who befriended you gave you these assignments?"

"Yes."

"Do you still work for him?"

"No."

"Why not?"

"Because I came to the conclusion this morning that if I'm going to continue killing people—and I am—I'm going to work alongside my father."

"Why's that?"

"Face it, you're not getting any younger. And I hardly ever get to see you."

"Can you still contact this man?"

"No. I'm moving forward. I *do* plan to continue seeing my boyfriend, though."

"The post-Rapture pet salesman?" I say.

"Yes."

"It's a scam, Kimberly."

"My code name is Maybe."

"Maybe?"

"Maybe Taylor."

I start to say something, but I'm sidetracked. "I like it," I say. "That's a great name!"

"Really?"

"Really. Where was I?"

"The boyfriend."

"Right. Your boyfriend's a con artist."

"True. And I'm an assassin. Which of us is worse?"

"Him."

We both laugh.

"So I can work with you?" she says.

"No."

Her face falls.

"But you can work *for* me," I say.

She breaks into a grin. "Really?"

"Really. But…"

"But what?"

"Let's not tell Mom, okay?"

ACKNOWLEDGMENTS

Special thanks to loyal Donovan Creed fan Rick Kocan, a great guy, fellow Penn State fan, and neuroradiologist, who told me about a special MRI machine that could possibly benefit one of the characters in my book. Thanks also to my brother, Ricky, who devoted an entire day of his valuable time to help me make this book that much better, and to Claudia Jackson, of Telemachus Press, who works tirelessly for me, and goes into her "above and beyond" mode almost daily!

DONOVAN CREED

DONOVAN CREED works as an assassin for an elite branch of Homeland Security. When he isn't killing terrorists, he moonlights as a hit man for the mob, and tests torture weapons for the Army. Donovan Creed is a very tough guy.

To discover more – and some tempting special offers – why not visit our website? www.headofzeus.com

LETHAL
PEOPLE
JOHN LOCKE

LETHAL
EXPERIMENT
JOHN LOCKE

SAVING
RACHEL
JOHN LOCKE

NOW
& THEN
JOHN LOCKE

WISH LIST
JOHN LOCKE

A GIRL
LIKE YOU
JOHN LOCKE

VEGAS
MOON
JOHN LOCKE

THE LOVE
YOU CRAVE
JOHN LOCKE